celebrating black women writers

Issue 3

EDITED BY:
Ianna A. Small

midnight & indigo
PUBLISHING

midnight & indigo

VOLUME 1, ISSUE 3
978-1-7328917-4-6

midnightandindigo.com

MANUSCRIPTS AND SUBMISSIONS
Whether you've already been published or are just starting out, we want to hear from you! We accept submissions of short stories and narrative essays written by Black women writers. View complete submission guidelines and submit your stories online at *midnightandindigo.com*. No paper submissions please.

Cover design by Asya Blue
Cover image: Sergey Filimonov/Stocksy United

Printed and bound in the United States of America.
First Printing November 2020

"There are years that ask questions and years that answer."

Zora Neale Hurston
Their Eyes Were Watching God

ISSUE 3

Editor's Note

As we head toward a much anticipated and (if I'm honest) welcome close to this chaotic year, compiling this collection has truly been a bright spot in this journey.

December marks midnight & indigo's second year as a contributor to this literary space; a celebration of the creativity and voices of the Black women who entrusted their dreams with ours. I'm humbled. As is the case with many journeys, we've grown and learned, stumbled and gotten back up...but most of all, continued to fortify our resolve to elevate our platform and serve the base of readers and writers that have formed our community.

In your hands, you hold our third lit mag baby. Three. The number that represents the whole. This issue, a collection of short stories and narrative essays written by nineteen Black women storytellers, reflects that triad; the beginning, middle, and end that all of us face as we learn and grow into our selves.

We witness reconciliations with identity, family, and self, alongside reminders that some life lessons will never allow themselves to be overshadowed. We meet women, ahead of their time, molding young minds or fighting for their definitions of freedom, and others for whom journeys back to basics, intrinsic and extrinsic, ultimately make all of the difference. Like many of us, these protagonists rise and fall, while finding ways to reclaim their power.

In **"The Outing"** by Itoro Bassey, a Nigerian-American woman navigates family, sexuality, trauma, and her need for independence. She is afraid to reconcile her past and discover who she is.

"Makers of Men" by Christine Hill explores the Black woman's burden in ensuring the well-being of Black men. In a community where boys are born and girls are created, two Sisters learn what it means to be part of their community.

A little boy is guided by his grandmother's love in **"The Easter Speech"** by Lori D. Johnson.

"**The Prell Sisters of Alabama**" by Ethel Smith is about three sisters who taught in the Black Belt of Alabama during the 1950s. Not only did they fight racism, but also sexism. Despite limited resources, these sisters teach their students, especially the young women, self-love and dignity.

Two lovers return to New Orleans to stoke the flames of their love affair, in "**The House on Dante and Belfast**" by Nikki Igbo. But not all is well in their private Southern paradise.

Set in 18th century West Africa, "**Alero**" by Noro Otitigbe is the story of a beautiful girl who marries the man of her dreams, only to be persecuted for her infertility. After many years of turmoil, she seeks salvation in the only haven she has ever known.

Thirty-year-old Tavia Calloway-Hurst is reminded of her spiritual strength after learning a painful lesson in "**Everybody Can't Come to Your House**" by Jasmyne K. Rogers.

"**Rooster**" by Michelle Johnson is based on the true story of the Kentucky Raid in Cass County, MI in 1847. The Black women who fought back against enslavers aren't typically spoken about. Mrs. Casey is placed at the center, fighting for her own freedom.

A Nigerian-American college student struggles with her identity in "**Coming Home**" by Vanessa Anyanso. While her name is Nigerian, she feels disconnected from her heritage and her parents. During a homecoming, she has an opportunity to form her own relationship with Nigeria.

Still coping with a recent breakup, Zuri has locked herself in the bedroom she shared with her ex-lover. When she receives a call from his wife, she learns that he has been dead for ten years, in "**How to Find a Husband**" by Jesica Lovelace.

In "**Heart Conjure**" by Stefani Cox, Sade and Delario seem to be the perfect match. They share a love for the Black spiritual tradition of hoodoo and ancestral/spirit-oriented practices. Eventually, however, they start to grow apart, and Sade has to find herself again.

After a series of disastrous relationships, Precious finds herself poor, alone, and suffering through the unrelenting misery of the bleakest winter ever in "**Roses On The Wallpaper**" by Ava Ming. Her daily emails to a stranger on a tropical shore provide a temporary escape.

In "**Yo—Excuse Me, Miss**," by Jennifer Celestin, Altagracia and Manny have a brief but powerful interaction on a city street.

Big Sister takes Little Sister from Englewood in **"A Day N the Life"** by Taylor Jordan. The school, the homework, Big Sister, all of them are different. Is this life really better, with its fancy pens and white people? Or should Antoinette ask Mama if she can come home?

A young man must decide what he is willing to risk to feel fulfilled in **"Donte's Choice"** by Shanda McManus.

In **"Congratulations, It's a Girl"** by Ambata Kazi-Nance, a young Black Muslim woman, estranged from her family, attends her older brother's wedding. A single mother with two young daughters, she wrestles with her life choices and feelings of judgment and failure from her family, as well as a new love interest she doesn't feel she deserves.

And we close with three narrative essays that speak to familial recollections and the ties that often bind.

After a 20-year estrangement, a daughter and her elderly father meet at a guest house in Zimbabwe to analyze the history of their painfully complex relationship in **The Postmortem** by Sekai K. Ward.

Impossible by Elizabeth Crowder explores memories of growing up with an anxiety disorder with a bipolar mother, within the framework of a near-death experience at a pool party.

Emotional absence is just as heartbreaking as physical absence, especially if it is a parent. **Looking for Papi** by María Elena Montero is about the space found to find and forgive a father for the ways he was absent.

As we head toward the new year and an expansion of our mission, we are so proud to have walked this literary road with each of you. If you're interested in reading additional stories, please check out previous issues, visit us at midnightandindigo.com, and follow us on social @midnightandindigo. Thank you for your support. Enjoy!

The Outing

The dream goes something like this:

I'm seated at a majestic banquet table gasping for air but doing my best to hide my asphyxiation. The corset I'm wearing is squeezing the dignity out of me, but since I look good, I bear it.

I see French macaroons, broccoli slathered in Velveeta cheese, fruit punch, Hamburg pizza, a pot of white sugar, garlic fries, biscuits, chocolate-covered donuts, evaporated milk, chin-chin, orange soda, petit fours, Lipton tea, red wine, Philly cheesesteaks, and a vat of sour cream on the dining table. These are the foods of my childhood and early twenties. I indulged in these foods for comfort. If I couldn't fix a problem, at least I could eat it. I still get cravings from time to time. Whenever I bite into sautéed kale with garlic, I catch myself thinking, *this is a buttered biscuit, this is a buttered biscuit, this is a buttered biscuit.* No surprise that I'm seeing a bounty of biscuits in this dream.

My family and our guests sit at the table. The women wear dresses with muted colors that are quite drab. The men banter back and forth, duking out who is most clever. Their collars are tight around their necks, and I fear they're choking but don't know it. Servants walk briskly about the dining hall to bring us food and drink. They look like blurs really, but I know they're there. My father sits at the head of the table, Mom's seated beside him, and there are random people I've never met which make me wonder if I should know them.

My father clinks his glass to propose a toast. He's donning a supersized afro that distracts me from his speech because amidst all these Victorian wigs, how's this afro going to pan out? He looks more suited to attend The Soul Train Awards or bite his thumb at the idea of a monarchy, but who am I to judge?

I stuff my face with a petit four, hoping to disappear.

Eating beats talking. I wouldn't even know what to say or how to say it anyway. A voice is a powerful impression, and I'm at a loss for which to use. Should I use the British English my parents speak in polite company or the pidgin they speak in exasperation? Should I use my standard American voice fit with a slight Bostonian mutter, or the voice I use when I'm about to molly wop somebody's ass? Maybe I should speak the language my parents spoke back home, though I don't know it; everyone assumes English isn't my first language anyway. Maybe I should use the voice I use with myself. Brief and resolute. I take a spoon of sour cream and eat.

"Lady Arit has a message to report tonight. I've heard from guests that it's a salacious secret. Though I detest scandal, I think it is best her ladyship reveal what's at hand here."

Everyone looks at me as if I'll be served for the main course.

"Yes, Arit," Mom says, taking a drink of wine, "we are most eager to hear this secret of yours. But before you divulge, allow me to share some advice. Nothing hides in the company of a prayer warrior."

The guests break into laughter as I eke out a few words. Mom shifts her eyes from me to the rest of the table.

"Don't fret over Lady Arit's peculiar disposition. She's taking precautions to ensure she'll relay her message wisely."

My father clears his throat and waves away the butler ready to serve the entree.

"Hurry now before our good meal goes cold," he barks.

I look at my reflection in the spoon and see it's an image of another woman. I refuse to name her, but she shakes her head and laughs through the brass. *Better tell them the truth, girl.*

My face heats up. My corset is too tight and the humiliation is near. The audience leans in to watch. I knock a pitcher of wine to the ground. The wine coats the floor until it becomes a pool of red. I scoop the wine and realize it's much thicker than expected and the smell is metallic. *Am I dead?*

I suddenly remember who I am in my waking life. If the wigs and posturing were out of the picture, I'm not sure there'd be much difference. I hold my knees as I cough, as the pool of whatever I'm swimming in rises. I yell, but liquid rushes in my mouth and down my throat. I wretch, trying to speak. *I can change.*

I wake up.

I began having this dream after Mom's phone call.

When she confronted me, she wouldn't say the word. She only

asked, "Are you someone engaging in woman to woman practices?"

The best I could answer was, "I'm not straight."

For a moment, she sounded relieved that the possibility of my dating the opposite sex wasn't ruled out. But I found myself irritated at her hope to make sense of me.

I pleaded with her that day, to my discomfort.

"Please don't say I'm completely this when I'm not sure I'm fully that." I couldn't tell if I was five years old or twenty-nine that day. Her voice had the authority of The Almighty, and what did I have? I sounded shrill and whiny, talking into the receiver, begging for validation. No bass, all flutter. It was a doomed conversation. There sat a grown woman who had forgotten herself. How sad.

I asked how she found out.

"Facebook. That picture you posted...are those women or men you're standing around? I can't tell. And why are you kissing that girl? Since when did you become...you don't look...nice," she said. "Were you hiding all this time?"

"No," I said. "I didn't think dating and hanging with who I want is such a crime."

Mom clicked her tongue.

"Dear, back where I come from, it is."

She calls the next day in a series of threes. Three times in the morning. Three times in the afternoon. Three times at night. Mom's obsessed with threes. Her fixation on the number started with her love of all things Jesus Christ.

Once she read the passage about how Jesus the Son belonged to the Father and the Holy Ghost, she believed everything had to belong to something. Three became her sweet number of belonging.

If she bought fruit, she had to buy the navel oranges, the purple grapes, *and* the bananas because they all belonged in the polka-dotted fruit bowl, together. If she was dressing me for church, she made sure I wore the itchy white lace dress, with the black Mary Jane's and that hideous striped sweater because, according to her, consistency in attire would put me closer to God. I've always feared her relationship with God; it seemed to override any need I had when trying to call her attention to what was happening under her nose. I would yank her arm, hoping she would look down, but she was always looking up.

For a year, I kept these worries at bay, but now my anxiety had taken over. Even now, I couldn't get her to look at me, and I didn't want to be another hopeless little girl tugging at her mother's pant leg. The best thing to do was ignore her, especially if she was preoccupied with a higher power.

Soon enough, I got a call that let me know exactly where I stand with her and God. *We didn't raise you this way.*

I begin sending her calls to voicemail.

In a moment of weakness, I pick up her call. I've watched plenty of bizarre movies where mothers put arsenic in your chicken noodle soup to collect life insurance, or sleep with your boyfriend, or beat you because they're threatened. This is the woman who picked up a gas station job working the graveyard shift to make a down payment on a house in a nicer neighborhood. She once hid in fear of a gruff man pounding the door, saying, "Come outside." *He had a gun,* she told me. *Thank goodness I locked the door.*

She was pregnant with me, and nine months later I lived in that house.

I take the call.

Remove that picture, please. They use social media back home, too. You'll never get to visit back home in peace if they know this about you.

I close my mouth and yell.

The following week, I skip her calls through pangs of nausea and gut punches that say, *This is my Mommy. I love my Mommy. This is my Mommy. I love my Mommy.* The phone rings. I stare. She leaves messages. Deadly messages. I pronounce the following week: The Week of Holy Terror.

Monday:
"Isn't it too much of the same thing? The same part bumping against the same thing?" she asks, knowing I'm not there. "You're such a pretty girl. Please, don't let it go to waste."

Tuesday:
She reads from the Bible. "Behold, this was the iniquity of thy sister Sodom, pride, fullness of bread, and abundance of idleness was in her

and in her daughters, neither did she strengthen the hand of the poor and needy. And they were haughty, and committed abomination before me: therefore I took them away as I saw no good."

Wednesday:
She sings.
Akwa convention
Odu ke edem eyon
Nyin ikwo iyun idara
Koro jehovah odong
Nyin Esit
Loose translation: I'm going to hell

Thursday:
"I've been thinking deeply about your cousin Minnie. I'm sure you've seen on Facebook that she likes to practice this woman to woman thing..."
I take a sip of tea (with a shot of whiskey) and wonder, *Where is this going?*
"Arit, you don't have to copy what Minnie is doing. Okay?"
I haven't spoken to Minnie in five years.

Friday:
She breathes into the receiver before saying anything. I wait.
"Maybe you've been away too long? You've been sounding different. Come home. Please."

Saturday:
"Should I tell your father?" she asks, though her question doesn't feel like an ask. I don't like keeping secrets. Arit, you have put your Mama in a terrible situation. Please fix your morality dear, I'm begging."
I scream at the phone. *YOU KEEP SECRETS ALL THE TIME.*

Sunday:
Her voice sounds frail.
"I love you."

"It's pure theater!" Nkechi eagerly listens to Mom's messages while eating a beef burrito. "She's an artist—but then again—what Nigerian Mom isn't?"

She hands back the phone. After nights of swimming in blood and drowning, I tell her everything. The phone call with Mom. The Facebook photo. The dreadful messages. Everything.

"What picture did she see, anyway?" Nkechi asks.

"The one of us at the parade where I had that rainbow skirt on."

"Got it." She nods, giving me a *that sucks* look. "No one should call you out for wearing a rainbow. How sacrilegious."

"I don't know what to do," I say.

"Do *you* boo." Nkechi sits back and swallows the last bite of burrito. "They don't pay for your flights home, and they don't buy your hair."

"I'm gonna keep eating carbs and sugar until I feel better."

"Not with your fibroids. Don't become a sadomasochist. Girl, just tell the truth."

"I'm not sure what truth to tell."

She flashes me a glance and takes a sip of Coke. "Yes, you do."

Nkechi. Life heightens when she's around. Like that day at the parade, it was already a day full of color and glee, but when she arrived, everything got brighter. She had a Grace Jones haircut with those three-dollar biker shorts she got at our favorite thrift store.

Folks danced in the street, and someone wrapped me in a magenta feather boa. Nkechi threw glitter, and for a good hour, I thought I was trapped inside an Instagram photo. Vivid. That's her. She makes reality an HD experience.

She's a heightener in her family too. Once, she barged in on her family during a prayer (her family prays like they're in the last days too) and said, "Look, don't expect any children 'cause nothing is coming out this canal and don't expect a husband 'cause marriage is for fools." She then pointed her finger directly at her parents as if she was the adult. "And don't try talking me out of it. We're in America and I'm gonna suck all the power I can from this country before I twirl back to my homeland."

After much silence, her mom—Mrs. Odegbami—became equally sassy and yelled, "Your very style of dress says that you are of the flamboyant variety. May you be washed in the blood of Christ as you make a mockery of everything I've tried to teach you." Then, she stood up and gave her daughter a kiss on the cheek. "I only pray that life isn't too hard for you. It's hard enough."

I wouldn't have believed this story, that her parents were this accepting, but she still lives at home, parties late into the night, changes her hair every two weeks, and smokes weed in the house (but only in her room with the window open).

Twerk on Friday. Energy healing on Saturday. Church on Sunday. Works for me.

I never understood why everyone expected Nigerians to be so dramatic until I met this family and thought I had entered into a Nollywood movie.

Nkechi's mom wears a long blonde weave looking like she's ready to faint (or wanting to faint) just cause life is *that* dramatic. The father is usually sitting somewhere in the corner, dosing off. All the while, people scuffle through the apartment from morning to night.

I grew up on the East Coast in a forest. Lots of quiet. Lots of brevity. Little color.

I look at Nkechi. "I wish your life would rub off on mine."

"What does that mean?" she asks.

"I mean—you know who you are. I worry so much that I don't know if I'm anything other than the worry."

Nkechi flashes me another look, a bit softer.

"I might tell them what I think, but I toe the line. I'll probably be that weird aunt everyone loves but secretly thinks, *wow, her life is ruined*. That's the part I've been cast in. I'd never do what you've done. Leave my family? No way," she says. "You're brave."

I laugh in utter disbelief.

"Brave?" I shriek. "All I feel is grief."

***

Where I come from, fervent prayer is the cure for all human folly. When Aunty Nancy heard about Uncle Emem's porn addiction, she sent him away (to a motel somewhere), packed up her rambunctious kids, and drove from Hartford, Connecticut, to my mom's prayer circle. It was held once a month for Nigerian women wanting to pray and link arms. They prayed morning, noon, and night that day.

I looked forward to this gathering 'cause it brought all of the children together. For one day, it was like Nigeria had descended upon our home. It was the Nigeria I watched on Nollywood, the one where I imagined people wearing perfume and cologne, where the women wore fancy head wraps, and large voices devoured the quietness. I'm not sure what Nigeria is when you've been living in the woods in another country for most of your life. But this Nigeria everyone connected with—the gregariousness and large displays of affection—was the one everyone seemed to recognize.

When my aunt visited, I relished the way us children were allowed to play freely. We'd tiptoe through the palo where our mothers linked arms and bowed their heads, rustle for food in the kitchen, then dash for the yard with a handful of chin-chin, howling into the forest. Our mothers were simmering with a mysterious something that none of us understood. I barely knew the home language—the language they prayed in—so what were they praying for, for hours on end?

We took any opportunity to leave the house and shout outside. Our voices echoed through the tall oak trees as we impersonated superheroes, Spiderman, Batman, Cat Woman, Storm, The Incredible Hulk; all of us wanted to save someone and play larger than life characters. If my father had seen me, I would have been spanked for not being a good girl, which to him meant remaining quiet and watchful. To have a daughter that dared to scream in a neighborhood where people walked their dogs, rode their bikes, and took note of everything was a travesty.

Thankfully, the women praying always seemed to keep my father and his temper at bay. He'd simply grunt, "Someone call me when the room is cleared," and retreat to his room.

After all the prayers, Uncle Emem returned a few weeks later, promising he'd give up porn and talk to the pastor about rededicating his life to Christ. The women were convinced their prayers had made the difference, but I think it was the fact that Aunty Nancy kicked him out, cut him off from his children, and was the breadwinner of the family.

He came back to the path of righteousness. That's what Mom said.

When Mom's father got diagnosed with brain cancer, she went to Nigeria to pray for him. Her entire family prayed every day at 9 am, 12 noon, and 3 pm. Grandpa died a month later and, for some reason, Mom still prays for his recovery. She believes everyone needs prayers, whether they're dead or living.

Mom prayed for my human folly too. When I was in high school, I took to wearing halter tops because that's what all the girls wore. From the day she caught me, I wore long-sleeved shirts in ninety-degree weather.

"You're a good girl. You're good," Mom said, taking me by the face with tears in her eyes. "You're good," she repeated.

That night I passed her room and stopped when I heard my name between words from the home language and bits of English. *Arit...make her good, Lord. Make her good.* My face grew damp with tears. A terrible feeling took hold of me, a feeling that someone had cast a spell behind my back. She gave God a message about who I was without any chance of me stating my peace. I realized that she had something over me, something that could very well kill me if I wasn't careful. Intention. She had a vision of me that always seemed to result in my being bad or being someone who either needed saving or was at risk of punishment.

I had a father that would slap me for any small infraction–not sweeping the steps right, daring to go to a friend's birthday party, burning the plantain, the list went on. It was like I couldn't catch a break, and all that time, I had thought it was my fault. But when I had caught her, my fears about her role in the matter were confirmed. She would most likely pray to God about my heathen tendencies before jumping in to stop a hand from slapping my face. That night I wanted to pray, not because I believed that God would save me, but because I needed someone to hear my side.

When she told God, "Make her good," I wanted to counter with, "I'm not bad." I realized that the primary authority figure in my life was not praying for anything that would free me from my pain, because she fundamentally thought that *I* was a pain. If this was her primary concern over my life–this prayer–spoken thousands of times to the Almighty, then no wonder why life was so difficult. I didn't know if I had the conviction to pray the way my mother did.

That night, my father and his rage faded into the background and my mother and her prayers came center stage. I guess she had a direct hotline to phone God in and say, this is who she is, but if anyone had asked me, I'd tell God: *This woman keeps interfering with my nature, and*

I don't know what to do.

But that night I didn't plead my case. I simply cried into my pillow, believing that if Mom thought I was bad, any cruelty I endured was definitely my fault.

I eat an enormous amount of macaroons with no taste. A bright fuchsia cookie ought to splash a berry goodness in your mouth. A tartness in the middle. A crunchy coat to sweeten the deal. I can't describe what nothing tastes like. It's more of a feeling. Imagine your mouth salivating, your tongue clicking against the roof of your mouth, sticky spit and a salty tongue wagging in your mouth and something fragrant (let's say a roast) under your nose that's teasing you, because however good it smells, you can't taste it.

I devour more cookies, eat through the blandness, grab the purple macaroon, then a green one, a tangerine, a yellow, a royal blue. I eat until I hear someone in the distance swear in my direction. It sounds like swearing, the timbre of it, disdainful. I'd rather eat through the blandness, but I hear her.

"How dare you blacken this royal house and your good name with such scandal!" Mom asks, taking a bite of Charlotte Russe.

I look down at my place setting. A pile of colored French cookies sitting on a plate. The fork is there, and I see the woman staring at me with a smile. *We all have to toe the line.*

She reaches her hand through the fork and begins reaching for my plate. *Hand me a macaroon, girl. This gonna be a long night.*

I give her a nice yellow one.

"Well," Mom says, "what do you have to say for yourself?"

I look down at the woman in the fork eating the macaroon. She looks to be wearing a Victorian dress with her hair now streaked yellow. *Just tell them,* she says. *Tell them you're different and that you're gonna stay at the table. Like me.* She chomps away, pleased with herself. *Doesn't this macaroon taste good?* she asks in delight.

I nod my head in agreement, not knowing why. Suddenly I get some taste from the bits of cookie in my mouth.

Dirt. It tastes like dirt.

Here are three things I don't like about Nkechi.

One. She's stupid. Or maybe she's psycho, but whatever she is, I find myself looking at her and thinking she's an absolute heathen. Nkechi's ability to heighten a situation can be a good thing or a bad thing. Usually, it feels mostly bad.

I'll never forget that time she walked the streets with lime green spandex, a crop top, and four-inch heels. She walked like this through the Tenderloin, the Haight, the Financial District, and the Castro. Past whistling men, past haughty women, past children, past police officers, past the wind, past the rain, past the sun, and past all reason. I offered her a coat, a blazer, a sweater, a scarf, but she refused.

She laughed that cackling laugh.

"All I have to do is be Black, pay my taxes and die," she said.

Does she have any idea who she is on this street?

"Stop worrying all the time," she said. "You got to raise your vibration in these streets and rise above the foolery, girl. Whether you live or die."

Two. She's a shit starter. Last week we were waiting at the BART, and a shifty looking man bumped into her. Nkechi snapped. "I'm standing here, idiot!" Now, it's eleven at night, we passed a man shooting up walking down the steps, and I have no interest in losing my life inside a train station. Nkechi knows this, but she doesn't care. This man doesn't scare me one bit. He wouldn't be the first shifty man I survived. But she—Nkechi—frightened me that day. She always carries pepper spray, a pocket knife, and a punch, wherever she goes.

The man's mouth is fowl and I'm sure I hate him. He starts talking. *Fuck you, you bitch this, you Black this, you c*!% this, you roach this...*

I send hand gestures and side-eyes her way, motioning for her to cool it, but she's ready to pounce.

"You don't want none of dis at this unholy hour. I will cut you!" she said.

He moved closer. No one's around and anyone nearby had headphones in, their faces buried in a book, or a cell phone recording the whole shebang.

"If he touches you, I'll hurt him!" I screamed. "Walk away. Please."

His attention turned toward me. *Fuck you, you bitch this, you Black this, you c*!% this, you roach this.* I wanted to throw him on the train rails. Hopefully only a few of his bones would break. What's a few broken limbs for someone who has the devil in him?

Nkechi laughed in his direction, that cackling laugh. "I will fling you across this platform. No joke, motherfucker."

He spat in her direction. Threw his entire head back to do it. The sticky yuck blob landed on her blouse. For a moment, she looked like a hurt kid. I stepped in. Slapped him. Twice. The shock sent him lumbering down toward the other side of the station.

"All the things we got to live with in this country," she said, rustling for a napkin in her backpack. "I should have kicked him in the balls. He lucky I'm not that fucked up on Jack. If I was, it would be over."

I searched my bag for a napkin to give her.

"You were livid," she said. "Did you hear what you were saying? With the way you were yelling, I thought you'd hit me too."

There was nothing to lose in that situation. I could hit him and no one would intervene, saying, "Don't hit *that* man, because he is so and so." But what Nkechi did that day...she could have got hurt. I could have slapped her for her recklessness, but I loved her. She a liability, though.

Three. She knows I don't like her. I can love a thing but not really like that same thing. I love her because she reminds me of home and she knows me from the inside out. She's gotten the closest, out of all of them, even more than any lover I've had. Up until three days ago, I was with someone named Jamal. A brother who always wears a five o'clock shadow. I considered sending a picture of us to Mom, hoping she'd accept this part of me. But then Jamal decided to pop up at my apartment with a Hamburg pizza. He was proud of his attempt at surprise but didn't see how destructive his behavior was. Any chance we had ended with that silly gesture. I don't like people in my space like that. Drop over and not give anybody notice? Who raised him? Truth is, I was waiting for a reason to dump him. Every time he commented on my looks—*you're great looking, you're beautiful and I really like you*—I wanted to hand him a cardboard cutout of myself and say, "Why don't you date her."

I told Nkechi this and she shook her head. "You take being alone to whole 'nother level, girl." Then she mentioned the girl I dated a few months back.

Sarah Jane. A high brow type from Napa Valley. She was trying to defy her father's expectations by working at a shelter. We were similar in ways and could relate to growing up in the woods. Nkechi hated how vanilla she was, but since it got me out on Friday nights, she soon approved. Sarah Jane and I met at some professional event. She kept calling, I finally gave in, and we began dating. Two months later, Sarah Jane wanted to take me for lunch with her best friend, Martha. I ended it a day later.

Nkechi asked why, and I said, "Never liked her name."

I'll never forget how my best friend grabbed my hand to give it a squeeze. "I want you to know that I like you *and* love you."

"Okay," I replied.

"I'm gonna like you and love you until you learn how to like and love yourself."

She's kind to me, and I love her, but I've never loved or liked a thing at the same time. And I certainly couldn't like someone who's half heathen.

To love a thing but not like a thing is perfectly sane in this kinda world. A world where people love but don't like, or like but don't love, or simply hate. I was a quiet girl. A shy girl. Meek. That was me. I didn't want to hurt nobody. I just wanted to be who I was, whatever *that* was, but in this trip of a world? I'm lucky. Lucky I'm anything at all.

It started with the day someone looked my way and said, *you're pretty.* It was a curse. Don't care what nobody says about the beautiful finishing first. It was. After that, the voices never stopped.

You pretty. Listen well. Pretty girls kiss men. Strong men. Big men. Like that one there. Wait. Not him. He White. He White-o. We don't want no wahala now. Too much to explain. Find a Black. No African-born Black. Won't understand you. Don't make him angry. If he hits you, it's over. Remember. Divorce is a sin. And you pretty. So pretty. Wait. You not pretty. Blacky. Lips too big. Hair too coiled. Ass too small. And you frown. Why frown? You pretty. So pretty. Wait. Why wear that? Show your legs. They nice. Wait. Why show your body? You a whore? Whore. Wait. You pretty. So pretty. Why wear baggy clothes? Wear a dress. Why you crying? Don't cry. You sensitive. Stop. Wait. I love you. Fool. Why you silent? Speak. Speak smart. Better than everybody. Not better than me. Sit down. What you say? Shut up. You too loud. No one will listen. You fucked up. For all of us. Wait. I adore you. Don't you know? Where's my credit? For loving you? You pretty. So pretty. Be strong. Kiss men. Pray hard. Sit in the corner. Amen.

The dream goes something like this:

I wake up and see there's no food or drink on the table. I know other people are there, but I only see my mother, my father, and the woman laughing in the spoon.

"Well?" my mother says. "What do you say for yourself?"

I look from the spoon to my mother, and then to my father.

"I love you, but I don't like you," I say. "Never have. And that's the truth."

Everyone disappears, and a plate of kale with roasted potatoes appears on the table. I know the kale is lightly sautéed in coconut oil and the potatoes are seasoned with turmeric because this is a meal I would prepare in my waking life. I'd prefer a chocolate chip cookie, but I realize that this is the meal that will keep me alive. A woman laughs in the distance, and I wonder if it is my voice I am hearing or the voice I've always been afraid to listen to.

Makers of Men

I was born of the sea. No woman was tormented to bring me into the world. All Black women are my mothers. And sisters. All Black women are me. And I, them. I was meant to be here. Called forth from the depths. Formed from earth and waves and clear midnight skies. My being was intentional. This place, this planet, this community, it needed me.

I remember the first time I heard a mother scream. I'd been sent out to gather special herbs from the garden. It was my first time. I was taken through the garden on several occasions, shown what each plant was, told what each was used for, but this was the first time I was allowed to pull from it.

Quickly, quickly, I was told, with a pat on the bottom. I walked toward the dwelling with a basket of sage, lavender, rosemary, rose petals, and witch hazel. A sister followed quickly behind me with a bowl of salt, harvested from the sea. We approached the dwelling but froze before we reached the entrance. The sound of a mother screaming pierced the air, stopping us mid-step. My hands trembled as we were pushed forward by an older sister.

"Hurry little ones," she whispered, "it's almost time."

"Time for what?" the sister next to me asked.

"Quietly." She nudged us through the partially separated curtain into the dwelling. "Bring that over here."

She directed us to an empty spot. I tried to keep my eyes forward, watching my feet as we tiptoed around the mothers standing in a circle in the center of the room, but there was another scream. I jerked my head toward the sound as the sister pulled the basket of herbs from my hands. I needed to get closer. I crawled between the feet of two mothers, trying not to be seen, and peered into the center of the circle. There was a mother, on her knees, her arms draped over the legs of the Great Mother who was holding her hands. Something was coming out of her. Before I could move any closer, someone grabbed me by my feet and dragged me from the circle.

"That is not for you to see little one. In time. Help me wash the herbs."

We washed the herbs I'd gathered in a bowl before mixing them in a larger bowl with the salt. The larger bowl was carried to the circle and handed to a mother who laid it at the feet of the Great Mother. Our work was done and we were escorted from the dwelling.

"What was that? What was happening to her?"

We were far enough from the dwelling that I no longer felt the need to whisper.

"Birth, little one. A boy."

"A boy?" We had boys. Little ones, big ones, and even bigger ones. Some were fathers. Some were not. "There was something coming out of her. What was coming out of mother? Why was she screaming? Is she dying?"

Tears welled up in my eyes at the thought of a mother leaving my world. There were so many mothers, each of them mine, but even losing just one, I couldn't bear the thought.

"She was giving birth to a boy. Bringing him into the world, giving him life." The sister knelt next to me and took my chin in her hand. "Boys come out of mothers and into the world. Do you understand?"

"But how? Babies come from the water." I looked intensely into her eyes. She looked intensely into mine.

"Maybe you're still too young to underst–"

"I'm not too young!" I stomped my foot. "I can understand," I said softly, digging my toes into the loose earth beneath my feet. "Just tell me *how*."

"You will understand when you become a mother." She pulled me into a tight hug. I could feel the heaviness of the explanation I was too young to understand. "Go play little one. Leave these things to the mothers."

Our community was sacred. It wasn't just something I knew, but as I got older, it became something I could feel. It was the way the sun smiled over us, in the sound of the waves tumbling over each other, in the sea salt air; it was in the way we came to be.

Boys are born, girls are created, I was told once.

It wasn't until I reached the age of cleansing that I understood.

It wasn't a sunny day. The sea was dark, as was the sky. The waves rolled almost as loud as the thunder, but there was no rain. Younger children, barefoot and giggling, ran up and down the stretch of land, chasing gulls trying to rest their wings from their fight against the strong winds. I woke to a throbbing in my stomach and wetness beneath me. I called for an older sister. *The Cleansing* was how the body emptied the womb of stagnant material to make the way clear for a boy to grow. It also marked the time when sisters would begin learning the ways of mothers. It would be a long time still before I would ever be a mother, but it was time to learn how to bring girl babies into the community; it was time to learn how boy babies were made. I was to learn so I did not bring either about before it was my time.

The sister took me by the hand and walked me through the community to the washing place. A pool of clear water surrounded by small baskets of dried herbs. She showed me how to gather the herbs, mix them in a bowl of water from the pool, and wash myself. I was to come to the washing place each morning and each evening during my time of cleansing and wash myself with the herbs. Then she showed me how to fold the cloth to wear in my garments to collect the material my body was shedding. She showed me how to wash the soiled cloth in the sea and how to hang it in the sun to dry.

She arranged flowers in my hair and tied a string of beads around my ankle, then walked me back through the community announcing, "Mothers! Your daughter has reached the age of cleansing!"

A seat was fashioned for me outside of my dwelling place, surrounded with flowers and seashells. Other sisters had reached the age of cleansing in the previous days and were seated in front of theirs as well, beaming and adorned with flowers. A large meal was prepared— bread, fish, and fruits of all kinds—music was played, we danced, we sang, we celebrated The Cleansing.

After my first cleansing was complete, I witnessed a baby girl brought forth from the sea. It was a practice all sisters must know before they became mothers. We must know how to bring girls into the world before we ever brought boys.

There was a cove at the East end of our community. It was forbidden to go there unless it was time for a girl child to be brought forth. Boys, men were never allowed there. It was a place deserving of respect.

On the day a girl child was to be called, the sisters who had reached the age of cleansing, and were empty, joined the mothers at the cove. At low tide, mothers and sisters stretched out on the compact sand, weaving flowers into bright green palm fronds as they talked and laughed and sang songs about the beauty, strength, and gentleness of woman. The fronds were then woven together into a large wreath and placed on the shore just out of the reach of the gentle waves. One by one, mothers and sisters sat down, cross-legged, and linked arms just beyond the edge of the wreath. An unbreakable chain.

I expected something remarkable to happen. Some flash of light from the sky or a heavy mist rolling across the water, but there was nothing. We sat in silence, eyes closed, for what seemed like an eternity, stretching our legs out toward the sea when needed and bringing them back in. Always bringing them back in. We sat until the rising tide covered our creation and reached our knees.

Then, one by one, just as they'd sat down, the mothers rose from the sand and the sisters followed. The Great Mother and her closest sister stayed at the cove's entrance, the rest of us walked in silence back to our dwelling places. There was no mandate for silence once we returned to the community, but speech didn't feel natural on my tongue for the rest of the evening.

The next morning the sisters rose early, and we busied ourselves with preparing for the new baby girl. A basket was woven for the new baby to sleep. It was lined with thick layers of cloth; a small handful of dried lavender was stuffed between the center layers of fabric to induce calm in the child. As the low evening tide approached, we made our way back to the cove. The mothers allowed those of us who were witnessing the bringing forth for the first time to walk ahead of the others. We greeted the Great Mothers and slowly entered the cove.

We could see something along the shore in the distance, just about where we'd sat the day before. We approached. Lying on the sand was the wreath of palm fronds, still green, but without flowers. And in the center of the wreath, a baby girl lying on her back, eyes wide open, hands stretched out, grabbing at the iridescent butterflies circling above her head.

I stood in awe as the Great Mother—the oldest in our community— lifted the girl child from the sand and wrapped her in the soft cloth that she'd worn over her shoulder. She kissed the baby's tiny feet before tucking them in, then led us home.

Asleep in the newly woven basket, the baby spent her first night in the care of the Great Mother. The next morning, she was given to a mother who had birthed a boy just three days before. The mother would feed and nurture both children. When the girl child was not feeding or sleeping, she would be with a sister or another mother. She belonged to all of us, and we belonged to her. She would learn from all of us, the ways of the community, the ways of sisters, the ways of mothers. I couldn't wait to introduce myself to her, but I knew I'd have to wait my turn. We all had a part in raising each other; we each had a different lesson to teach the younger sisters, just as the older sisters each had a lesson to teach us.

The girl child, Obsidian, grew quickly. She was just as strong as she was beautiful. By the time the boy child reached three years old, Obsidian was nearly six, and by the time he reached ten, she was a teenager. She fed him, clothed him, helped him learn to read, and showed him where to find the best fishing spot. Of course, the men taught him the actual fishing, but Obsidian was obsessed with the water and she knew it well. For a time, she took over the role of the mother, as all sisters did with boy children. Girls grew much faster than boys and accepted the responsibility of teaching them as soon as the boy's mother was ready to bring another one into the world. This was the way of the community.

Obsidian's boy was called Roca. He was strong like she was, but much faster. She could outsmart him any day, but had a difficult time keeping up with him when he didn't want to be kept. After Roca's mother had birthed her third boy, her man decided to leave the community. No one knew where the men went when they left, except the men. No sister or mother had ever bothered to follow them—there was too much attachment to the community—too much to do—and the men always came back eventually.

The men had their secrets just as the women did, but boy children, just like girl children, were not allowed to know those secrets. Roca became angry when his mother's man left. He'd grown very attached to the man, following behind his every step, eating when the man ate, sleeping when the man slept, fishing when the man fished. And when the man left, Roca cried because he could not follow. He cried, he yelled, he smashed whatever was in his way, then he ran down the beach as far as he could go until his legs ached. Obsidian found him some time later lying in the sand, staring up at the darkening sky.

"He left." Roca sighed.

"I know." Obsidian sat next to him, digging her toes into the sand. "You know he'll come back, right? The men always come back."

"But where do they *go*?" he whined. "Nobody would tell me."

He scratched at the small scar above his eyebrow. A reminder that roosters should neither be chased nor caught.

"And they never will." Obsidian pulled the small boy into her lap and twirled her fingers around chunks of his curly hair. "You'll find out when you become a man. And you'll probably leave your woman and your boy too, and your boy will cry for you just as you cry now."

Obsidian sat with the boy until the sun dipped low beyond the sea. Then she pulled him to his feet, and they walked back to the community. She helped him clean the mess he'd left in their dwelling, brought him food to eat, and settled him onto his mat as his eyes became heavy and he could no longer hold his bowl. Then she strolled out to the edge of the community and sat staring out at the dark water. Soon, I joined her.

"I want to know too," she said in a low voice.

"Know what?"

"Where the men go." We were silent for a moment, eyes focused on the expanding darkness. "I don't know if I want a man." She looked at me then. "I don't know if I want to make more boys."

I sighed heavily.

"Boys are our burden. They are our blessing. If we refuse them, we die; if we refuse them, the community dies."

"It doesn't have to!" She turned to me and took both of my hands in hers, fire blazing in her eyes. "It could be just us! Mothers, sisters, daughters. Just think of it, how much better it would be!"

"And who would hunt?" I asked, pulling my hands from hers. "Who would build dwellings? Who would defend the community? We wouldn't survive without them, Obsidian. You know that!"

"We would! I would!" She softened. "We could learn to do all those things. We're strong. We could defend ourselves. We could fish. Build. Hunt. We could if we wanted. If we *tried*."

"Come now." I stood and reached a hand to her. "You need to rest, child. It's been a long day, you chasing after Roca and all."

She took my hand and pulled herself up from the sand.

I wrapped an arm around her and pulled her close as we walked back toward our dwellings. "I know it's frustrating, scary even, but they're good, you know. And you don't have to take a man if you don't want to. And you don't have to make more boys if you don't want to. We'll name you 'Keeper of Hens'!"

She giggled at her new title.

I kissed her forehead and nudged her toward her dwelling, where Roca was snoring loudly. "It won't last forever, little sister. I promise."

"No," I screamed, "she said I didn't have to!" I was tied to a chair, surrounded by mothers and sisters. There was a man too. Part of me knew it wasn't real. I was dreaming. I could feel the haze. But I could smell, and hear, and see everything so clearly that it outweighed the haze. Overpowered it. My feet were secured to the legs of the chair, my hands to the arms, nails digging into the soft wood. My shirt was torn, exposing my belly. The mothers and sisters held hands in a circle around me, the man stood just beyond my knees. There was something hidden in his palms. The dwelling smelled of salts—the kind made by the ocean and the kind made by the body. "I don—" I coughed. "I—" I couldn't get the sounds out. I don't want this! She said I didn't have to! I want to be Keeper of Hens! Tears fell from my eyes as I gasped for words that wouldn't come. The man knelt between my knees, showing me what he held in his hands. A seed. He smiled as he pressed it hard against my belly. "We are the makers of men," he said, removing his empty hands from my flesh, "there is no way out." I could feel the skin on my stomach beginning to stretch, I could feel the bulging begin. I looked down and then back at the man, but I couldn't look him in the eyes. I could only stare at the scar above his eyebrow.

The Easter Speech

Even though his favorite afternoon cartoon hadn't been on more than a good three minutes, the little boy didn't waste any time leaping up and running out to the porch when he heard his Big Mama Cora Lee call, "Porter! Porter, come on out here and show Miz Nan how well you know your Easter speech."

Five and a half-year-old Porter had been named after his Big Mama's people. "You were named after folks who knew they were about something. Always remember that and don't ever let nobody try and tell you different," is what she'd made a point of clarifying for him ever since he'd gotten up to be some size.

There wasn't anything Porter wouldn't do for his Big Mama Cora Lee, and instinctively he knew the same held true for her when it came to him. Her love reigned as his sword and shield in a world that seemed hell-bent on taking him out at every turn, and by the same token, he represented for her that long-awaited glimmer of hope.

His eyes glued to the old woman's smile, the little boy stuck out his chest and cleared his throat before reciting by heart the words he knew would only make her dentured grin stretch that much wider.

Upon his finish, Miz Nan rewarded him with a boisterous round of applause and her trademark cackle of a laugh.

"Good gracious a life!" she said, turning to Porter's beaming Big Mama, who sat in the rocking chair next to Miz Nan's with Porter's little sister, Theresa, balanced atop her darkened knees. "Cora Lee," Miz Nan went on, "I do believe this here granbaby of your'n is gone make all of us right proud one of these days."

Porter's Big Mama pulled Theresa, who everybody called 'Sweet Tea,' back into her lap before she said, "I've been trying to tell you, Nan. Yes ma'am, this here boy is gonna be something else. Truth be told, I knew it the first time I laid eyes on him." She pointed to a spot between her breasts and drew a circle near her heart. "A little voice right in here told me, *Cora Lee, this boy here, he the one. No doubt about it, he is the one."*

As if to further confirm the point, Sweet Tea threw up her chubby arms and fat little fists, and like some touchdown inspired cheerleader at a homecoming football game shouted, "Yay Po' dah! Yay!"

With his baby sister's cheers and the laughter of the two old women ringing above his head, Porter fell into his Big Mama's embrace and quietly indulged in a grin of his own. He drew in a deep breath, sucking in as much of his grandmother's scent as his five and a half-year-old lungs would allow. Her smell, a near-perfect blend of butterscotch and caramel mixed with just a hint of rubbing alcohol, served simultaneously as his source of power and his salve for the disruption that lived way down deep in his soul.

***

Big Mama Cora Lee hailed from the old school—the type that did her best, prayed on the rest, and wasn't never scared. A giant of a woman, her mere presence often invoked the fear of God in others. Or, at least, that's the way it seemed through the pecan tint of her grandson's admiring eyes. In actuality, she towered all of four-foot something and was what the old folk called illy-formed at that. But if being born with a pair of knees going in one direction and a set of feet veering off in yet another made Cora Lee a handicap, she didn't know anything about it.

What might have stopped a lot of folk, most days, barely even slowed her down.

Her toughness, coupled with her generosity of spirit, was the stuff from which many a "hush your mouth" legend had been woven and spun. To the gangster wannabe who'd made the mistake of stopping on the sidewalk in front of Cora's Lee's porch, only to start yelling and cussing at one of his homies on the other side of the street, she'd politely said, "Young man, I'd thank you kindly to take that mess on way from 'round my porch and these here babies."

Instead of offering up a shamefaced, "Yes ma'am," the slack-jawed teen had summoned the gumption to grab his crotch and say, "If you know what's good for you, you'll shut up talkin' to me and take your old, Black ass back in the house!"

Rather than heed the threat, Porter's Big Mama had stood up and shuffled over to the porch's railing where she'd peered down at the youth and said, "Is that right?"

The boy, obviously unaware of who he'd been messing with, had said, "What? You think I'm playing? You'd best mind your own, you old ugly, knock-kneed, stank-tail, bow-legged witch!"

Porter, who'd been waiting for his cue to make a run for it and praying he wouldn't soil his pants in the process, watched as his Big Mama tightened her grip on the porch's railing, spat into the yard and said, "I got yo' witch, baby. Umm-hmm, sho'll do."

Something, either in her voice or in her eyes, had finally pulled the boy's coat to the invincible nature of his opponent and pushed him toward the more sensible option of backing down. He'd strutted off, still cussing and calling Cora Lee out her name.

And having sealed his fate, he wasn't but two steps from the corner when the delivery truck swerved through the turn, jumped the curb, and slammed into him.

"Don't worry none," is what Cora Lee had said in response to her grandson's startled gasp. "That fool ain't no deader than he was while he was standing up here talking all that junk, like somebody crazy."

And she'd called it right, of course. The "accident" didn't kill the young man, just maimed him and broke him up so bad that for a couple of months or more, he kind of halfway wished he was dead.

***

Rather than go back inside and finish watching cartoons, Porter pulled Sweet Tea from his Big Mama's lap and walked her to the four concrete steps that led up one side of the porch. His arms stretched forth as both a guide and a precaution, he stood in front of the little girl and watched as she plopped on her diapered behind and eased down the staircase, just like he'd taught her.

Porter took serious the task of looking out for his two-year-old sister. After all, "Keep an eye out for Sweet Tea," is what his Big Mama had been telling him since the day baby girl had first shown up in their lives. "Don't let her get hurt and try not to let nobody mistreat her," is what Cora Lee told him time and time again. "But if something bad should happen, you make sure you come back and tell Big Mama all about it."

According to Porter's Big Mama, if she kept an eye on him and he, in turn, looked out after Sweet Tea, in the end, everything would be all right.

Porter didn't doubt the soundness of his Big Mama's theory; he knew as long as he didn't venture too far beyond the boundaries of her gaze, no harm would dare come to him. The altercation he'd witnessed between her and the foul-mouthed teen had proven as much. But what the child feared was that the old woman's gaze didn't stretch quite far enough.

As he'd grown older, he'd become more and more in tune to both the shortcomings and the vulnerability of the one person his Big Mama repeatedly failed to mention on her "keep an eye out for" list.

"What about Mama?" is what a troubled Porter had asked Cora Lee one day. "Who's gonna see after Mama?"

After a few seconds of dead silence, the old woman had pulled her grandson into her arms, mashed his head against her bosom, and told him, "Don't you worry none 'bout your Mama. The Good Lord is watching out after all of us—your Mama included. You hear?"

Porter had heard her all right, but something about the way she'd said it had given him even more reason to wonder.

He pulled a couple of toy racecars from his pocket and handed them to Sweet Tea before he sat down on the step beside her. He loved sitting on his Big Mama's porch. Even with its proximity to a heavily traveled street and its steady stream of pedestrian passersby, he felt safe and more at peace there than he did most anywhere.

But if his grandmother's porch with its rickety rocking chairs, chipped paint, cracked flower pots, and worrisome bees represented young Porter's idea of heaven, then surely that other porch—the urine-stained one with the flea-infested sofa; the one that sat in front of the duplex his birth mother insisted he and Sweet Tea call home—surely that porch had to be about as close he ever wanted to get to that place folks called hell.

At the duplex, rather than tenderly rendered words of praise, support, wisdom, and comfort, the little boy's ears were routinely assaulted by curses and insults; a never-ending litany of the coarse and the profane that generally grew worse as the sun sank behind the building-topped horizon. Even in his bedroom with the door closed, the windows shut, and the covers pulled up over his head, Porter could still hear them out there.

In between the *bitches* and the *mf's*, the *heifers* and *the ho's*, it was pretty much *nigga, nigga, nigga,* all night long.

***

"Yeah chile," Porter heard his Big Mama say, "last Easter was something else! I declare if me and these here children didn't near 'bout miss making it up to the Lord's house altogether."

"Oh, that's right," Miz Nan said. "That piece of car of your'n started acting up, didn't it?"

His Big Mama chuckled and said, "Umm-hmm. Wasn't nothin' but old man Lucifer trying to keep me from hearing my baby give his speech. But we sho'll fixed his devilish tail right good, didn't we Porter?"

Porter's memories of last Easter were a jumbled mix of sights and sounds, sensations, and emotions. When he closed his eyes and squeezed them tight, they all descended upon him, one after the other: the chocolate bunny, jellybeans, and colored eggs in his basket; Sweet Tea in her pink ruffles, white lace, and black patent leather.

The gentle bite of his starched collar; the annoying pinch of the brand new tie knotted against his throat; his eager climb onto the stage and self-assured deliverance of the Easter speech his Sunday school teacher had given him—the one meant for a child twice his age. All of the *Yes Lords! Amens!* and *Hallelujahs* that had broken out afterward, the rough handshakes and firm pats on the back that came from the pastor as well as all the gray-haired deacons, all the congratulatory hugs and kisses of the church mothers, their voices echoing his Big Mama's chant and forever burning themselves into the far reaches of his subconscious, "I declare if this here boy ain't the one, sho' nuff, y'all. Lord as my witness, I do believe this here child gone be the one."

But what Porter remembered most were the tears of pride and joy he'd seen in his grandmother's eyes and the way it had made him feel. Even though the little boy didn't fully comprehend what all being "the one" entailed, what he did know, beyond a shadow of a doubt, was that for his Big Mama Cora Lee, he would willingly be that and more.

Miz Nan laughed, then said, "Brother Lucifer is sho' nuff something else, ain't he? Always showing up someplace, looking to stir up trouble."

Porter's Big Mama grunted. "You got that right. Ain't hardly gonna be no trouble that don't have his ole mischief-making behind right up there in the midst of it."

"You know though, Cora Lee," Miz Nan said in a more serious voice, "seem like that just might be the problem with a lot of these children out here nowadays. For some reason or another, they act like they don't even recognize the devil when they see 'em. Shoot, most of 'em ain't even halfway trying, don't look like to me."

Porter turned his face toward his Big Mama to better sop up her every word, like he might a saucer full of cane syrup with a thick, buttered biscuit.

"Crying shame ain't it?" is what he heard her say over the creak of her slow-moving chair. He watched as she rocked and traded looks with Miz Nan before fixing her gaze against his.

"The way I see it," she went on, "the devil done already gone and put himself a nice sized down payment on a lot of these young people's souls. And that being the case, shouldn't hardly come as no surprise that ain't too many of 'em got the will nor the wherewithal to wanna shake him loose. Kinda hard to fight what you done already made so much a part of your life, don't you think?"

***

Porter's stomach flipped into a series of knots when his mother walked through the door of his Big Mama's house that afternoon. Had anyone bothered to ask, the little boy would have been quick to say that he wasn't nowhere near 'bout ready to go.

Truth be told, he never was. Very little joy marked the life he led at that awful duplex on the other side of town. His mother, Ava Marie, saw to that. If not screaming curses, whispering threats, or raring back to smack his ass, she was, for the most part, ignoring him altogether. Ava Marie owned the distinct dishonor of being the most unlovable creature Porter had come to know in the brief span of his five and a half years.

Still, he couldn't help but love her just the same. Not once had it ever occurred to him to do otherwise. Even so, on that particular day, rather than his mother, Porter had hoped his ride back to the duplex would have come courtesy of his mother's boyfriend, Rickey.

Porter liked Rickey. Even though he looked the part with his baggy pants and the trademark cap he kept cocked over his brow, Rickey

40

stood out from most of the others his mother had let saunter in and out of their lives. For one, he made Porter's mother laugh a whole lot more than he ever made her cry. Even more to his credit, he knew how to act when he came around Porter's Big Mama.

The little boy never would forget the first time the two of them met. A grinning Rickey had come bouncing up on Cora Lee's porch and, after introducing himself, had spun around and traded dap with Porter.

"Yo!" Rickey had said, bumping fists with the boy. "What up, my nigga?"

Porter had already grown accustomed to Rickey's boisterous ways and playful nature. He wouldn't have thought twice about the exchange had his Big Mama not risen from her seat with a frown and said, "I ain't meaning for you to take this the wrong way, but much as I appreciate you doing this here child's Mama the favor of coming by and picking him up, it might behoove you to know that his name ain't nigga. It's Porter." She'd spelled it out. "P-o-r-t-e-r. And that's with a capital P, I might add. Now, I don't suspect I'll be needing to repeat myself, will I?"

"No, ma'am," Rickey had said. "Didn't mean no offense. From here on out, Porter it is."

Later in the car, Rickey said, "Porter, man, your Big Mama is a trip. Remind me a whole lot of my own. Take it from me lil man, having a grandmama like that will help your butt steer clear of a whole lot of trouble."

Ever since that day, Rickey had gone out of his way to show Miz Cora Lee the respect she rightfully deserved. Had he been the one picking up the children that day, he wouldn't have had a problem waiting until they'd eaten their dinner. Matter of fact, he would have pulled up a chair in hopes of enjoying a serving or two himself.

But the person who stormed through Porter's Big Mama's house that day appeared to have only one thing on her mind—getting out of there as fast, if not faster than she'd come in.

"What's your hurry, chile?" Cora Lee said as she watched Ava Marie snatch up Sweet Tea with one hand and the baby's bag with the other. "These chillren ain't even had they dinner yet. At least let me fix 'em a plate to take with 'em."

Ava Marie shook her head. "Can't Big Mama. Don't have time. Not today. Gotta go see a girl 'bout a book for class."

Porter knew good and well that was a lie. But he knew even better than to try and call his mother out on it. In the last year or so, he'd come to understand that for Ava Marie, lying to Big Mama had become yet another entry on that long list of those things she didn't know how not to do. Unlike Rickey, she seemed to feel little regard for the woman who'd taken her in and raised her, when at age twelve she'd been all but abandoned by her blood kin. Ava Marie thought nothing of lying to or talking bad about the woman who frequently kept her children on short notice and who made seeing that they were safe, fed, in good health and properly clothed, her number one priority in life.

"A class?" his Big Mama said, her face brightening into a smile. "Well, why didn't you say so in the first place then?"

Cora Lee's belief in education ranked right up there with her unshakeable faith in the Almighty. Seldom, if ever, did the old woman bypass an opportunity to encourage Ava Marie to go back to school. Nothing pleased her more than to think that the hardheaded gal she'd tried to raise had finally heeded her advice and had taken the steps required to make a better life for herself and her offspring.

But for Porter, who knew that his mother's urgency had nothing to do with any ole book, "pleased" didn't even come close to describing his feelings. While his stomach cried out for the fried chicken, cornbread, macaroni and cheese, and greens his Big Mama had cooked especially for him, his eyes watered at the thought of yet another night of dry cereal and stale bread, washed down with a glassful of tepid tap water.

On stealing a glance in her grandson's direction, Cora Lee pulled out one of the handkerchiefs she kept tucked away in the pockets of her oversized, flower-print housecoat. "Come here, baby," she said, beckoning the boy toward her. "Let Big Mama help you get that out your eye."

"Ain't nuthin' wrong with that boy," Ava Marie protested. "I told you Big Mama I can't be here all night. I got folks to see and thangs to do."

"Oh, this ain't gonna take but a minute," Cora Lee said. She cupped her hand beneath the pouting little boy's chin and winked at him before she pressed the handkerchief to his face.

"Tell you what," she said to Ava Marie as she dabbed. "Why don't you go on and take a peek at the cute little dress I bought Sweet Tea to wear on Easter. Go on. It's in the closet right next to the front door. Me and Porter be out there directly."

Ava Marie heaved a sigh, then swung around and marched out with Sweet Tea and the baby bag in tow. With a smile on her lips, Porter's Big Mama handed him the handkerchief before busying herself about the kitchen. The boy marveled at the quick, fluid movements of Cora Lee's swollen hands and gnarled fingers as she wrapped several pieces of chicken in foil and packed a couple of heaping scoops of the macaroni and cheese into an empty margarine container.

While she worked, she told him, "You mash this up real good like I showed you before you give any of it to Sweet Tea, you hear? And I'm gonna save these greens and this here cornbread for y'all to eat on tomorrow. Now, let's get on out there 'for your Mama commence to fussing again."

They hurried into the living room only to find a mumbling Ava Marie pacing from one side of the opened front door to the other, like a house-trained dog in dire need of letting out. Porter peered into his mother's face and realized in an instant that a part of her had already gotten up and gone.

He squinted up at his Big Mama to see if she knew. While the fact that it ever happened at all existed within the realm of those things left unspoken between them, in the past Porter had always known Cora Lee to be quick about honing in on and addressing her daughter's periodic leaves of absence. Her standard approach to what had only recently become a problem, generally involved summoning an excuse to keep either Ava Marie or else the children in her presence just a little while longer.

But this time, rather than attempt to thwart her daughter's pressing desire to leave and take her babies with her, Cora Lee grinned at the fidgeting girl and said, "First you went and got yourself a decent paying job. Now you done turned 'round and gone back to school. I suspect you be done come back to church before you know it."

Ava Marie rolled her eyes and said, "Please, I wouldn't count on it." With her face pinched and clouded into a frown, she grabbed Porter by the hand and said, "Come on here boy."

"Wait now," Cora Lee said.

Porter, who just knew his Big Mama had finally caught on and at any second would come to his rescue, closed his eyes and sent up a silent, *Thank you, Lord.* But his reprieve lasted only as long as it took for his Big Mama to open the closet and pull out his windbreaker.

"It's gotten cool out there," she said, on leaning over and helping the child into the jacket.

"Big Mama, I wanna stay here with you," he said, balling his fingers around the handkerchief she'd given him earlier.

She chuckled and said, "What you still fretting 'bout, huh?" She pulled the handkerchief from his fist and shoved it into a pocket of his windbreaker before she kissed him on the forehead. "You go on with your Mama. And later on, after you've eaten your dinner, I want you to practice your Easter speech. You hear?"

"Yes ma'am," he said, nodding his head and biting his lip to keep from betraying his true emotions.

He took the paper sack full of food the old woman thrust at him and followed Ava Marie out to the car. On climbing into the back seat, he helped his mother get Sweet Tea fastened in next to him before turning to his Big Mama Cora Lee and extending her a sad wave goodbye.

The little boy's head bounced and rolled against the torn backseat as the car lurched forward and sped off down the narrow street. He waited until the car had barreled around the corner and hit the main thoroughfare doing anywhere from ten to fifteen miles over the posted speed limit before he decided to risk incurring his mother's wrath by leaning forward and asking, "Mama, where we going?"

She glared at him through the rearview mirror, but before she could respond, Sweet Tea started whining. Ava Marie dug a sucker out of her purse and passed it to her son with instructions to unwrap it and give it to his baby sister.

The boy frowned and said, "Big Mama say Sweet Tea too little to have this kind of candy. She say—"

"Hey!" Ava Marie yelled, taking her eyes off the road and jerking her head toward him. "Ain't I done told you 'bout quoting Big Mama to me? Big Mama ain't never had shit to say that I wanted to hear, all right?"

Porter knew whenever his mother used that tone of voice, he'd best get quiet and make himself as invisible as possible. That particular shift in tone warned him that she'd gone from not being herself to being someone, if not something else, altogether.

Besides, a few minutes later when Ava Marie clicked off the radio and started humming "Wade In The Water"—that song they sang at Porter's Big Mama's church whenever somebody was about to get baptized in the name of the Father, the Son, and the Holy Ghost, the boy didn't need to ask any more questions. He knew where they were headed—the same place they always went whenever Ava Marie got a notion to start humming that particular tune—the river.

* * *

Their treks to the riverside had begun in earnest in the early Fall of the year just passed. Ava Marie would drive them to a spot on Mud Island where the unobstructed waters of the Mississippi rose up to kiss the bluff city's dark bottom.

The first couple of times, they'd only parked and sat in the car. Porter remembered the swell of wonder and delight he'd initially felt upon gazing out over the never-ending stretch of water. But in the weeks after that, the novelty of the experience had slowly lessened, due in large part to his mother's insistence on moving them closer and closer to the river's uneven edge with each subsequent visit.

The little boy knew as soon as the car skidded to a stop on the bank that evening, his mother wouldn't be content with simply staring out across the water or tossing in a rock or even dipping in a toe. Still, he did what she told him. He unbuckled Sweet Tea from her car seat and helped her out. He pulled off his jacket and shoes and tossed them atop the car's warm hood. He seized Ava Marie's hand and walked alongside her as if he didn't sense the gentle stir of something other than spring in the air.

Obedient, mannerly child that his Big Mama had raised him to be, Porter, without protest, followed Ava Marie to the point along the bank where the solid sureness of grass and ground gave way to the slick uncertainty of mud and water. Even though his mother's hum of the baptismal hymn grew louder with every slosh-filled step, Porter knew what she had in mind had little, if anything, to do with the promise of salvation.

Still, he couldn't find it in himself to balk until he felt something reaching for him beneath the deceptive calm of the river's ever-rising surface. The thought of some nameless boogie man, some unknown beast hiding out down there, waiting to do Lord knows what, sent Porter's teeth into a chatter. With the sudden rise of the boy's body into a float, the faceless something beneath him fastened a grip against the bare bottoms of his feet and tugged. Fear rattled the boy's vocal cords in a screeching yelp. He snatched his hand away from his mother's and propelled himself backward through the cold, murky depths.

"Come on here, boy," Ava Marie said. She stopped and adjusted Sweet Tea against her hip. "What you scared of? It ain't deep."

Porter shook his head and sputtered, "Big Mama tole me not to be playing 'round no water. She say she gone see 'bout getting me and Sweet Tea some swimming lessons this summer."

Ava Marie laughed, resumed her wade and said, "What you worried 'bout Big Mama for? Ain't like she ever got to know."

When the boy heard his baby sister whimper and call his name, he couldn't fight his inclination to start back toward her. After all, he'd promised his Big Mama he'd always do his best to see after Sweet Tea.

"That's right, Porter," Ava Marie said, bobbing up and down like a water ballerina on point. "Come and get Sweet Tea. Come on. Just a little bit further."

But when the grin on his mother's face slipped just enough for Porter to get a good look at the distorted face lurking behind it, he stopped creeping forward and said, "Uh-uh, you ain't none of my Mama. I recognize you. You ain't nobody but the devil! Uh-huh, and all you trying to do is keep me from saying my Easter Speech."

Porter splashed back toward the bank, and upon freeing himself from the river and looking back, all he saw floating atop the water's now still surface was the red sucker Sweet Tea had been holding in her hand. In that moment, a chill, like none he'd ever experienced before swept over him.

His chest heaving and his body racked by a series of violent shivers, he stumbled to the car and wrestled on his jacket. As he sank down in the grass and struggled to hold back the sob he felt building up inside of him, he kept hearing Rickey's voice telling him, as he often did, *All right Porter, ain't no need for all that sniveling and carrying on. You gots to man up and stay hard with it, dog. You know what I'm saying? You gots to man up.*

But when Porter pulled the handkerchief from the pocket of his jacket and brought it to his nose, Rickey's voice gave way to the familiar scent and sound of one older and wiser.

As Cora Lee's presence wrapped itself around the slump-shouldered little boy and the water welled up and spilled from his eyes, he sought comfort in something he remembered her telling him once.

Ain't no shame in tears, baby. No sir, none at'll. Even Jesus wept.

The House on Dante and Belfast

Lana remembered the first lie she ever told Samuel. On that day, a 70s radio station played loud. Steely Dan was done with dirty work. Joni Mitchell had fallen for a sweet-talker and needed help. The words and their melodies added another level of thickness to the humidity that Lana was finding hard to tolerate.

"You should turn off the stereo before you run down your battery," she said. "Quiet is better."

They sat in Samuel's truck bed and ate crawfish tails for brunch. Lana didn't want to litter the streets with the shells, but Samuel assured her the heads, claws and all, were biodegradable.

"Let's leave it all right here on the street," Samuel said, his lips glistening with crawfish juice. "Anyone who sees them will think of laughter in City Park and slow dances in the middle of Bourbon Street. Any New Orleanian would appreciate that."

Lana didn't remind Samuel that neither of them was New Orleanian. She never said that her romance with the city died a little more each time she visited. She saw the greyed remains of another boil farther down the road, and it looked less like a celebration and more like a mistake. Above their heads, four strings of orphaned Mardi Gras beads hung in the branches of an oak tree. A breeze made them collide with each other and fall away.

"How was your drive from Houston?" Lana asked, as she pictured him behind the wheel with eyes fixed responsibly on the road as he crossed the Horace Wilkinson Bridge and made his way closer to where she had been waiting at the house on Dante and Belfast. She thought of the drives they'd taken to Lake Pontchartrain after lazy afternoons spent in the big bedroom on the second floor, back when college exams and weekend parties were their only concerns.

She lifted a tail to her lips. She could not find good crawfish in Los Angeles. If she and Samuel could just spend the next three days together with as many shrimp po'boys and spiced potatoes as possible, she would return West with no regrets. To Lana, that wasn't greed; it was appreciation. A deep appreciation for what she didn't have elsewhere. She didn't think about what waited for Samuel back in Houston.

Samuel dismissed her question as he leaned forward and touched his index finger to her lower lip to outline the curve. Lana smiled as she was reminded of the previous night's activities. New colors on the moon's face, swings around Venus. She wanted to sing him a Roberta Flack song. She wondered if he'd heard it before. She never got to ask this second question because his cell phone rang.

Lana noted the powdered sugar in his voice and knew it wasn't his mother or sister on the other end. Samuel turned from Lana, his eyes down, his body curled into a whisper.

Lana regarded Samuel while trying to ignore the words he spoke as she dug around in the crawfish bag. The spicy juice from the tails found a paper cut on her left hand. She fought the urge to swear. Instead, she grunted as she brought her sore hand to her mouth before thinking better of it. She decided to swallow the pain along with more crawfish.

When she tried to peel another tail, the meat crumbled before she could separate it from its shell. Viewing the lost meat as an omen, she stood and tossed the tail into the middle of the street. Muttering a few curses, she thought about how good it would feel to simply punt the entire bag out of the truck bed. Samuel glanced back at her.

I'm so sorry, he mouthed.

Lana spat her reply, "There will always be more crawfish."

She climbed down from the truck and went back inside the house. She sunk onto the couch where she and Samuel had made love for the first time under an itchy plaid blanket. Rain had fallen that night. The earth had sighed. They'd discovered new definitions for the words "sticky" and "gumbo." Afterward, they held each other with the blanket cast aside and the couch poised in a permanent shrug.

The day after that encounter, they'd tried to avoid each other in Chemistry lab. It had been a lost cause. The house, where he'd lived with his two roommates, became key to their Voodoo ritual. Whenever he summoned, she came. Whenever she telephoned, he invited. Her presence there became so common that he'd presented her with a toothbrush and her own drawer. But they never admitted to being an item. Perhaps the spell they'd cast had been incomplete, she pondered.

Ghosts of his touch made her turn toward the window to watch him place the phone in his pocket and walk toward the house. She felt her face relax. Her body remembered the here and now of him. No phone call could ever take that away. She thought it but didn't believe it.

The screen door slammed behind Samuel. He sat next to Lana and leaned in to kiss her shoulder. She smelled Hugo Boss on his t-shirt and recalled how hazy morning sunlight had found them just hours earlier with his leg across hers and her drool on his chest.

"Does she know you're here with me?"

"She knows your name and who you are—." He stopped as if interrupted, though Lana said nothing. She let the air between them expand and go limp. The next few moments wrapped around her throat and squeezed.

"I've told her how I feel about you. I've explained that we have a connection," Samuel continued. Lana noted the shift on Samuel's face. Spiders second-lined around the inside of her belly.

"What about David? Did you give him back his ring?"

David. Lana retracted at the sound of that name from Samuel's mouth. She didn't like when Samuel spoke her fiancé's name, because it sounded like a curse or an insult on his lips. She preferred Samuel use a faceless, soulless pronoun. Lana replied by showing Samuel her naked left hand.

"Well, it's over between me and Ermite. We're just friends. That's all we ever should have been. You know how I feel about you. You know what I really want." Samuel spoke this as he rubbed the vacant groove on her ring finger. It was a tactile confirmation, as if he didn't trust his own eyes. She didn't tell him that the ring was wrapped in a silk scarf, stuffed in her purse upstairs. She kissed him to remind him of pralines and other sweet things in their immediate future.

Lana imagined she would tell more lies during later encounters. Lies to conceal the various happenings of that day between them. Whispered lies. Lies of omission. Not the kind of plump, white lies that float by without harm, but rather the kind that teem and stretch and swirl. The lies would gather on the floor, pool around their feet, rising up to pull their love affair under. But on that day, Lana was okay with not being honest about David.

"Why don't you come take a shower with me and wash my back?" Lana walked a few steps away from her lover before stopping to remove her shirt and toss it back at him. She let the loose pants she wore, his favorite pair of khakis, fall to her ankles as she cupped her breasts and continued toward the stairs.

"I know we said we'd see a movie, but I've got other things I could show you," Lana teased.

The matinee at Canal Place could wait along with the rest of the curved city. The city could be damned for all Lana cared. There wasn't enough time to contend with streetcars and I-10 traffic or any other Big Easy truths that could give her an excuse to come to her senses. She ran up the staircase and called to Samuel below.

She said, "Let's just be for as long we can."

Once in the bathroom at the top of the stairs, she gazed at herself through the water spots on the mirror. When Samuel appeared behind her, she cast her eyes downward and kept her secret. Samuel turned on the shower and the bathroom became a fog.

He placed his thumbs just inside the band of her underwear, pulled them down below the curve of her bottom, and let them drop to the floor as he kissed his favorite spot on the nape of her neck. He then reached around her to place his cell phone on the sink while Lana began to remove his clothes.

"I want to be under the water with you until our fingertips wrinkle. I should bring the stereo in here. Wait one second."

Samuel left the bathroom and Lana turned toward the sink. Glancing down, she noticed Samuel's phone was unlocked. Her fingers flurried to access his text messages. Her heartbeat mimicking the drummer they'd heard on Congo Square as she found the last electronic missive sent just minutes ago from Ermite...

Looking forward to feeling your body against mine again.

Lana reverted the screen back to the way she'd found it and felt the urge to wash her hands. Tears welled as she rinsed suds from her palms and fingertips, but she didn't allow them to fall. She was no lower ninth ward levee; she would not break.

When Samuel returned to her in the bathroom and pulled her naked frame into his own, she decided she would keep that secret as well, and hoped the house on Dante and Belfast would withstand the inevitable storm.

Alero

Acojah, son of Chief Odafe, was well known throughout the nine villages along the Toru Beni River delta. It was said that the gods loved
his mother so much that they ordered the very best carver to craft his
body and face out of a mountain, and when they finished, they placed
their creation inside her womb. His frame was sturdy and tall. And
when he spoke, everyone looked on the ground to see if gold dust fell
from his tongue so they could pick it up. As a young man, he was
praised for bringing honor to his Uhrobo people by wrestling the great
Deinabo, an eminent warrior of the Ijaw tribe. Everyone feared Deinabo, for he was massive like the Iroko tree, but Acojah lived up to his
name and rose to the challenge.

    The bout between the two warriors began on the first day of the
Ohworu festival. It was the fiercest battle the land had ever seen. The
men fought almost to their death. When Acojah pinned Deinabo's back
upon the fertile red soil, his victory sanctioned his status as the greatest warrior amongst the nine tribes of the delta.

Alero, daughter of Edema, was an exquisite young woman. When she
strolled through the market with a calabash full of water on her head,
her body moved from one step to the next, as if she carried a ripe mel-
on in each hip and a tiny diamond wedged into each of her heels. Her
copper skin glistened as if the sun melted itself onto her bones. Her
bright smile could be seen from one end of the market to the other.
Alero's large white teeth flashed like elephant tusks when she spoke.
Everyone, man, woman, and child was transfixed by her presence. The
people swiveled their necks to watch the voluptuous girl as she walked
past. They would stare, mesmerized by her girth and exceptional beauty.

    As the only daughter, she diligently performed her filial duties. She
cleaned and she cooked cheerfully for her five junior brothers and her
parents. Alero was praised for her luscious ogbono stew. She would

grind the seeds of a ripe ogbono fruit and use it to make a gigantic pot of stew, enough for all nine villages. She liked to cook and serve everyone with a beaming smile. The villagers often gathered around to taste her delicious meal. Sometimes, while they all ate and laughed, Alero would sneak into the forest and sit upon the roots of a grand oak tree. She enjoyed being alone in the forest while she listened to the birds sing to her. Alero delighted in watching the snakes slither in the soil, and she loved feeling the snails glide between her toes. In the forest, the eldest daughter did not have to cook clean or smile for anymore. The young beauty could just sit and revel in watching the world around her. Every so often, Alero could hear the leaves of the grand oak tree whisper sweet love psalms to her. She would sing sweet love songs back to them and laugh when the leaves tickled her ears.

When it came time for Acojah to decide upon his first wife, there was no debate. He had his eyes upon Alero since his triumph at the Ohworu festival. Everyone was certain that she would be a loyal wife and bear many strong children. The villagers commented that had she a strong back to help the farmer with his ever-expanding cocoyam farm.

Their wedding was a sight to behold. Chief Odafe gave his son a generous portion of his most arable land and built a large compound for his favored heir. For seven moons, the people of all the nine villages gathered around the compound to celebrate their union. They feasted on the most succulent meats and drank the finest palm wine. Alero's mother and father rejoiced and boasted about the tremendous bride price their daughter had garnered for her family.

"I am simple fisherman," the proud father exclaimed with a belly full of palm wine and sweet meat. "Alero, I am fortunate to have you as my beautiful daughter. My firstborn and only girl pekin. Indeed, you live up to the meaning of your Itsekiri name—the earth where she walks is truly soft. It opens up to send blessings to you and to those around you.

Everyone cheered, and the father turned to his new son. "Acojah, my son, I have given you my very best seed. She, in turn, will give you her very best fruit." And with that, Edema planted the seed of an ogbono tree in the center of the couple's new compound. The villagers cheered and clapped and drank to the father's benediction.

Many seasons passed and everyone began to wonder why the strong man and beautiful woman had not yet produced. It was prophesied that their offspring would bring pride to both of their people. However, hope began to wane as time went on and the new wife was not with child.

The young girls at the market would snicker and point at Alero.

"If I were the wife of a great warrior, I would have had many of his children by now," they would jest.

The men mocked the wrestler, "What kind of warrior cannot even conquer his own wife."

The new wife, aware of all the comments, wanted to respond by saying, "Leave me be!" Instead, she ignored them and fulfilled her obligations as a humble, hard-working first wife.

Each evening, the farmer returned to his compound, forlorn and ashamed. The cook comforted her husband with her savory stew.

As the seasons went by, the married couple settled into their routine. The warrior returned home defeated. The cook comforted him with her signature meal. It did not take long for Acojah's once-powerful, chiseled body to grow soft. His flat, firm torso ballooned into a rotund belly. His firm, square jaw was now hidden underneath fleshy, round cheeks. When the wrestler mounted his wife, his plump stomach smothered her, and with each thrust he made inside her, he let out a loud, long fart. Acojah's farts emanated from so deep within his being that he could feel its journey. The fart would begin in the vacuous hollow of his navel then move upwards through the inner channels of his midsection, then the heavy wind wrapped around his spine and journeyed downwards until it finally exited from his tender anus with the gusto of a hellacious tornado. The toxic fumes of his flatulence permeated throughout the entire compound, and Alero spent hours the next morning burning herbs to eliminate the horrible odor. This continued for many moons.

One day as Alero was returning home from the market, she saw her mother from afar. She ran to greet her. She had not been to visit her parents since her wedding day, and upon seeing her mother, she realized how much she missed her family. As Alero approached her mother, the old woman hurriedly walked away from her daughter. It was as if she did not recognize her own child.

"Mama, it's me o!" Alero called out with open arms.

"Please," the mother said. "Please go. I cannot be seen with you."

"But mama, am I not your child?" Alero pleaded on her knees.

Her mother stopped walking and turned to the distraught daughter.

"A child is supposed to bring joy to a parent," she said. "Since your marriage, all you have brought is shame to your family. If you could see how all the women in our village mock your father and me for the disappointment you have caused, you would know not to approach. They say the ogbono tree your father planted on your wedding day will soon bear fruit, yet you remain fruitless. They say we accepted a high bride price knowing that our daughter was a dry cow. Acojah's Clan has sent people many times to collect money from us. We give them what little we have."

The mother suppressed her tears as she spoke. She turned her back and walked away from her daughter.

Alero did not know what to do. She cried, and she felt ashamed. The girl wanted to run and hide deep in the forest. But she wondered if the grand trees in the forest would also turn their branches away from her.

The girl sulked as she plodded toward the compound. As Alero trudged along the road, she noticed all the other women walking past her. It seemed as though each of them was traveling with a heavy step and a swollen belly. After all, what is a child for? Alero thought to herself. If I birth one, they will say one is not enough, you must birth another. If I birth a boy they will say, now you must birth a girl to help with the farm. If I birth a girl, they will say now you must birth a boy to carry on the family name. It is like a sullen song that goes around and around and never ends. No one will ever be content with the tune I play.

When Alero arrived home, she noticed the roots of the ogbono tree had indeed begun to emerge from beneath the soil. Soon it would be overflowing with produce. She looked down and rubbed her flat stomach. At that very moment, Alero decided that she would never bear any children. Not for Acojah or for any other man.

On the first day of the Ohworu festival, many harvests after the couple's union, Acojah was to wrestle Deinabo again. All the villagers came from far and wide to witness the match. They knew that despite the grappler's weight gain, he was still an outstanding fighter. And they were right! The battle began, and at once, Acojah lifted Deinabo high above his head; he threw him to the ground and pinned him down on his stomach. The match seemed to be over before it even began. Acojah was confident that his victory would soon be declared. Suddenly, as Acojah had Deinabo kissing the earth, he felt a grumbling in his stomach. He instantly knew that this was one of his great farts making its way from deep inside his body to the outside world. The wrestler tried with all of his might to clench his buttocks, but he could not suppress the unyielding wind that overpowered his robust frame.

All of a sudden, he let out a resounding, guttural fart. The gas from his body released itself with a sound like that of a pregnant elephant moaning with labor pains. The earth surrounding the grapplers began to rumble from the vibration of the flatulence.

Deinabo quickly heaved Acojah off him, spun him onto his back, and pinned his opponent to the ground. The crowd roared with laughter and covered their nose. Not only was the flatus loud, it smelled like sour goat meat that had been left in the sun. The harmattan winds blew the horrible odor through the crowd. The warrior felt all of his pride leave his body as quickly as the fart left his body. Deinabo flattened Acojah against the earth as he defeated the fallen fighter. The humiliated warrior buried his head in shame.

The cocoyam farmer stormed back to his compound full of rage. He saw his barren wife squatting near the fire, chopping peppers for the ogbono stew. He rushed toward her, grabbed her by her hair, and began to scold her.

"You witch," he exclaimed, "you have turned me into a woman. I am no longer the powerful warrior I used to be. It is all your fault!"

The husband started to beat his wife.

"My love," Alero cried, "please do not be mad. Let me make you some ogbono stew. You will feel better."

"It is your stew that has done this to me," he declared.

The wrestler struck his wife repeatedly. Everyone from the compound came to watch. Nobody came to Alero's aid. Instead, they all nodded their head and agreed that she was indeed a witch.

Alero tried to run, but Acojah grabbed her. He held her by her neck and squeezed her tight. She struggled to break free from her husband's grip, but he was far too strong. She reached toward his face and gouged at his eyes. The hot pepper residue on her fingers burnt his eyes, and he was forced to release his barren wife.

"Woman, I will kill you!" he shouted.

Alero ran from her husband toward the neighbors, but they pushed her away.

"Get away from us, you witch," they exclaimed.

Alero saw her husband pursuing her, wielding a giant club. Seeing no other recourse, she ran toward the hot fire and dove into the only source of solace she had known all her life—her soothing ogbono stew. Everyone gasped as her beautiful body melted into the stew. The wrestler stood in disbelief.

The entire compound surrounded the fire and shook their head.

"Poor, pathetic girl," they lamented. "Now she will never bear children for the great Acojah."

Acojah ordered the village children to carry the large pot filled with stew and woman deep into the forest and pour it into the soil near the roots of a grand oak tree.

When the children returned to the compound, they presented the pot to Acojah. He ordered them to scrape all the residue of his deceased wife and the stew onto the ground, then wash the pot clean. When the children finished, Acojah ordered his mother to prepare ogbono stew for all nine villages.

"That woman was not good enough for you," the mother told the son.

"Mama, please cook for me. I want to remember her one last time," the son told the mother. "Tomorrow, you will find a new wife for me."

All the villagers tasted the stew and agreed it was more flavorful than ever before. They all concurred that indeed the spirit of Alero now flavors the ogbono stew very well.

"Ogbono stew has always tasted delicious," Acojah declared as he licked the food off his fingers, "but now, with the spirit of Alero in every bite, it is even more tasty."

Late at night while everyone in the compound slept peacefully, Acojah tossed and turned. A rumbling in his body would not allow for a peaceful slumber. It was not the same rumbling he felt from his farts. He knew this was a different kind of restlessness.

Acojah heard a faint moaning sound coming from outside, echoing through his compound. He followed the wailing sound to the back of his home then toward the forest. As he approached the center of the forest, the yowling grew louder and the words grew clearer. It sounded like Alero, weeping. Acojah pursued the trail of the moan all the way to the grandest tree in the woods. It was dark, and all he could see was the vague shape of the trees, yet he heard Alero loud and clear.

Acojah, see me Acojah! Alero lamented.

Acojah bent down upon his knees. He placed his ear to the ground so as to hear her more clearly. Suddenly the wailing stopped.

"Alero," the remorseful husband cried, "is that you? My wife, please forgive me."

Silence. Acojah, desperate to hear his wife's voice again, laid the entire front side of his body down flat upon the earth. His broad frame blanketed the roots of the tree and the cool dirt.

"Alero," he cried, "please sing to me."

Silence. Acojah began to weep, his tears sank into the soil. Then, just as he felt he could not weep any longer, he heard it again. Alero began to sing.

Acojah, my husband, she whimpered.

Acojah clawed his fingers into the dirt. The roots of the tree slowly raised from beneath the dirt and bore themselves deep into his stomach. Acojah's belly began to inflate like a mother baboon in heat. He could not stop it. Nor could he move. Alero sang to him as his belly swelled.

My husband, you shall know how it feels to carry the heavy load of a woman. You will crave my sweetness for all your days.

You will devour me, yet you will never be full. My spirit will roam through your body until the wind carries me away. You will crave my sweetness again. I will come to you again.

Alero stopped singing then, and the whole forest stood still. The branches ceased to sway, the snakes halted their slithering, and the birds held their beaks tightly together. Acojah remained with his face pressed against the ground, not knowing whether to stand and run or to sink deep into the earth. Stricken with fear, Acojah's body went limp and he fell asleep cradled by the forest floor.

Acojah woke the next day to the dazzling sun shining directly into his eyes. He rolled to his side with great difficulty, then he placed his palms flat on the ground to prop himself upright. As he bent over, he noticed his stomach was larger than ever before.

"What is this?" Acojah cried. "I thought I was dreaming! What has happened to me?"

Acojah ran out of the forest in outrage. When he arrived at his compound, the village children pointed and giggled at him.

"He has the belly of a pregnant woman," they chided.

They had seen wealthy men with enormous stomachs before but never quite like this. Acojah's stomach was perfectly round, and it protruded directly in front of him as if the stomach wanted to announce itself many days before Acojah arrived. The protuberance caused the skin on his torso to stretch, so there were very many horizontal lines that led twisted paths to his navel. The children asked him if he was carrying the child of a zebra.

Acojah ran to hide.

For many moons, he refused to be seen. He did not eat, yet his belly did not return to its previous state.

One day when Acojah's mother came to visit her son, she noticed the ogbono tree that Alero's father planted was starting to bear small fruit. She rushed back to her husband.

"My husband," she cried, "look how our son remains childless, yet the tree of that cursed woman's Clan begins to produce fruit. What must we do?"

Chief Odafe marched to speak to his son at once, but Acojah was too ashamed to face his father. He remained concealed inside his home. Chief Odafe stood next to the ogbono tree and spoke with a booming voice so that his disgraced spawn and all the neighbors could hear.

"My eldest boy," he began, "you are the heir to my wealth. You are my greatest gift. I see you hide in shame. Know that I am your father and you are my son. There is nothing that can make me turn my back away from you."

With that, Chief Odafe exited his son's compound, and his wife followed.

The next day, the people from all nine villages gathered for the Ohworu festival. A crop of young new warriors would fight to be seen. The sprightly grapplers fought for their life, they kicked up dust and groaned and grunted as they wrestled one another with all their might. Then, just as the victor was about to be declared, a gust swept through the crowd.

Dust blew toward everyone's face, and when the fog cleared, they saw Acojah with his towering frame walk toward them like a poised lion. He wore a white wrapper which sat below his grandiose stomach. He walked heavily, his head held high and his back straight. A multitude of gold and coral necklaces rested upon the protuberance of his midsection. The women swooned as he walked past them. The crowd parted as he strutted through the center of the ceremony.

By the next festival, Acojah was the proud father of a son, and his new wife was pregnant with a second child. Acojah, like his father, became a very wealthy man. He had many wives, though none as beautiful as Alero, who bore many sons. Like their father, his sons grew to crave ogbono soup. They would each marry a wife who knew how to pluck the fruit from the tree within their father's compound to make a fine meal for them. Like their father, all of Acojah's sons were cursed with chronic flatulence. The villagers affectionately referred to the men of Acojah's bloodline as pruu pruu men. They relieved themselves shamelessly, and they carried their enlarged midsection as a symbol of wealth and pride. Hence, to this day, the many male offspring of Chief Acojah of the Toru Beni River delta now known as the Niger River delta carry their swollen stomach and their constant flatulence with the same pride as their forefather. And with each fart that escapes their body, whether great or small, one can hear a faint whisper like the song of a delicate young woman. *Alerrrooo, Alerrrooo, Alerrrooo.*

Everybody Can't Come to Your House

"I told you about letting everybody come to your house, Tavia."

Tavia Calloway-Hurst could barely see her mother. Her vision was blurred from the tears that stormed her face. She sat in the middle of the hardwood floor surrounded by hair. Her hand shook uncontrollably. She heard *clink!* every time she drew a shallow breath.

She looked down at her trembling hand and noticed she was still holding the pair of silver shears. She wailed again. Her mother gripped the sides of her burnt-orange dress to kneel and join her in her space. Janey Lee Calloway took the pair of shears from her daughter's hand and placed them by her side. A weapon she selected to use on herself.

Janey took inventory of the hair scattered on the floor. Her daughter had long, thick hair that touched the small of her back. Folks would often compliment Tavia on her healthy mane and wished her hair could replace their own.

Thirty years' worth of hair wildly abandoned on the hardwood floor in a matter of fifteen minutes. Fifteen damn minutes. The sun beamed outside but refused to enter the red brick house that sat on the corner of Kennedy Street. The yellow and white polka dot curtains were drawn, and the blinds were open. Darkness filled the room despite the sun being out.

Janey Lee heard her daughter's scream from her front porch. Tavia stayed three houses down near the field. She had yet to confirm whether the scream was audible, or if she just inherently knew something pained her daughter.

While Janey Lee sat with Tavia, she knew it was the latter. Thick hurt covered the layers of Tavia's moans. Janey Lee closed her eyes. That type of pain was familiar. Inherited.

The silence was thin under the hurt that suffocated the room. It entered without an invitation. Made a home in Tavia.

Janey knew.

Janey also knew that silence was necessary. Although the hurt overpowered the silence, silence equated to strength in this moment. There were acres of words that Janey Lee could allow to escape into the space they occupied, but they would welcome anger too soon.

The silence welcomed vulnerability.

Tavia wailed, whimpered, moaned, and became mute in that space. This was important. Important for healing.

Janey Lee realized she was in a daze—staring outside at the sun that would not come in. She looked over to her right to find her daughter with her knees to her chest, rocking back and forth. Tavia wanted to stand but was unsure of her strength, so she laid down on the cold black and white tiled floor instead. Sprawled out. She closed her eyes to forget.

"Mama," she whispered, eyes still closed.

Janey Lee placed her left hand atop of Tavia's right hand. "You've got to get up from here, Tay."

Tavia opened her eyes as her Mama pulled her up.

"Go sit down over there, Chile. I'll run you some water."

Janey Lee pointed at the couch as she walked in the direction of the kitchen, not the bathroom.

Janey rummaged through Tavia's spice cabinet until she ran her hand across sea salt and sage. She drew the curtains closed as she walked across the hardwood floor to the bathroom. Janey hummed. A deep hum that erupted from the pit of her stomach. She turned the knob on the tub. Warm water gushed from the faucet. Janey Lee placed sea salt and sage in her hand then sprinkled the mixture into the tub.

Her humming transformed into a soft song.

She pulled her daughter from her space on the couch, undressed her, and guided her into the tub.

"Relax, honey. The water will help you."

Janey walked back to the living room to sweep her daughter's tresses. Sweeping and humming. The streetlights flickered, and she heard mothers calling their kids in the house. She smiled as she remembered a sweet memory.

Six-year-old Tavia spun around the front yard smiling at the sun. Soon, she retired from spinning, and her short, chubby fingers made acquaintance with the earth. She dug until the dirt reached her knuckles.

"Ma!" she called onto the front porch that faced her back.

Janey rolled the last section of Sylvia Jane's hair in a soft roller and gently patted Sylvia's shoulder to let her know she was all done. Janey rounded the flowerbed and stood next to Tavia, whose hands were firmly planted in the earth.

"Ma, if I put sunflower seeds in the ground, will they grow?"

"Yes, but you'll have to dig deeper."

Janey Lee knelt down and unearthed the top layer of soil. She hummed a medley. Tavia giggled, revealing her toothless smile. Janey loved to hear Tavia's giggles. It made her world all right.

As night approached, they were covering the sunflower seeds. Tavia got up quickly from her place on the ground and twirled while chanting, "I'm going to have sunflowers! Some flowers from the sun!"

Flowers from the sun. Tough soil, but the sunflowers bloomed, and so did Tavia.

Janey Lee returned to reality when she heard the whirring of water going down the drain of the tub.

"Tay, you okay?" she called out to her daughter.

"Yes, Mama. I'll be back up front shortly."

Janey gazed at the cherry moon before closing the front door. She sat on the gray L-sectional adorned with sunflower pillows. Photo frames decorated the glass table next to the couch, photos of younger Tavia and Janey, Tavia and her siblings, and Tavia and her husband.

Just as Janey Lee was staring at Tavia and Jarrod's photo, Tavia sat next to her. For a moment, Tavia forgot and attempted to swoop her hair behind her ear.

"I had to cut it, mama," she whispered softly. "You know I had to. She had been all in my hair."

"And in your house," Janey Lee added.

Tavia nodded.

"You felt something was off about her a long time ago."

"I did. Just thought it was safe to give her the benefit of the doubt." Tavia wiped the tears that welled in her eyes.

Janey Lee felt like she was talking to her thirteen-year-old, who wore bright eyes and dressed the world in good clothes until that day when life introduced her to an alternate world where folks wore masks for both justifiable and damaging reasons. She had always been open. Vulnerable. Giving. Willing. Hopeful.

"It's never safe. It's never safe to dismiss your intuition, darling. The more you listen to it, the stronger it becomes. The stronger it becomes, the more you are protected."

"Everything is changing. How am I supposed to deal with this? Heal from this? How?" Tavia's voice quivered.

Janey Lee closed her eyes and drew long breaths until the color blue painted her mind. "Everyone doesn't have good intentions, no matter how they appear. Start trusting your intuition. I know you made your mind up that Lela was safe, but you knew something was off. You felt it in your knower—in the bottom of your stomach whenever she was near or doing your hair."

Tavia shook her head and raked her fingers through her hair.

"It will grow back—healthier and longer than before. You intuitively knew you had to get rid of her energy."

Tavia quietly wept.

Janey Lee surveyed the room that wore flowers from the sun. It felt different.

"I need to cleanse my house," Tavia said. Janey Lee nodded. She knew Tavia felt the uneasiness in the room as well.

"I cannot believe Jarrod, though. We've been married five years, Ma. Damn!" Tavia buried her face in her hands. Sadness invited anger.

Janey Lee remembered the day Jarrod Hurst proposed to her daughter. They had been rising in love since their freshman year of college. Three years later, he proposed to her at the family fish fry. Tavia loved family, and she loved a good fish fry. Janey Lee's older sister, Mayra fried catfish and hushpuppies like no other.

Right before Tavia took a bite of her fish sandwich mushed in wax paper, Jarrod got on his knee. She said yes and forgot all about her fish sandwich. That was a first for her. Mile-wide smiles covered the backyard while Betty Wright's "No Pain, No Gain" filled the space.

Everyone was happy for Tavia and shouting, "Lawd have mercy! Tavia gettin' married!"

"Tavia, you have gifts. After what has transpired, you will utilize these gifts more. That gal couldn't get to you because you are divinely protected. She wanted a piece of you, your energy. Although you are a highly vulnerable woman, you are powerful on a spiritual level. That is the reason you are so vulnerable."

Tavia pondered Janey Lee's words. She had always felt different. Too sensitive. At times, when Lela came over to do her hair, she greeted her with a warm hug and happiness, but as soon as Lela's fingertips touched her scalp, she felt anger, bitterness, and sometimes jealousy. She dismissed the feelings because they never stayed long.

It was a while before Lela met Jarrod, and it was not on purpose. He had gotten off work early to surprise Tavia for their anniversary. She scheduled an appointment for Lela to do her hair because she was not expecting Jarrod home until seven. They were carried away in conversation when Jarrod opened the screen door.

"Baby!"

"Hey there." He smiled.

Lela stood, masked with a smirk and curling iron in hand. Tavia introduced them. They finished the conversation while Tavia felt feelings brewing under their disguises.

"I have some sage, Palo Santo, Florida water, and sea salt. I'll cleanse the house tonight."

Janey Lee gently held her daughter's hand. Tavia offered a faint smile.

"Has Jarrod been back?"

"No, I have not seen him in days; I am sure he is still out there doing lines."

Janey Lee looked into Tavia's eyes. Tears were no longer welling.

"Your home is your sanctuary, akin to your soul. Everybody can't come to your sacred space. After you smudge, focus on healing. Anything that brings you closer to healing, do that. All the tools you need are within." Janey Lee got up from her space on the sectional.

"Need me to drive you home, Ma?"

Janey Lee chuckled. "Girl, you act like I live a long ways away. I don't mind the five-minute walk."

"Okay, Mama. Thank you, and I love you."

Tavia hugged her mother tightly and stood on her front porch as she watched her hum her way home. Once she heard her mother's front porch screen door creak, she closed and locked her home.

Time to cleanse and heal.

Janey Lee awakened from her slumber and looked at the clock that read 6:32 a.m. She stretched, grabbed her house robe, and walked to her kitchen. She opened the blinds and smiled.

Tavia was in the front yard on her knees, humming and digging. She did not notice her mother looking out the window at her. The trees and sunflowers danced to the rhythm of the wind, a sign that the ancestors approved.

Tavia planted the seeds and covered them with the earth and her tears.

Tough soil. Tough world. But the sunflowers would bloom again, and so would Tavia.

She spun and twirled until everything blended. She felt connected. It felt so damn good to her soul. She felt a sense of flight without ever leaving the ground. She felt like her six-year-old self in that moment. Ready and open to receive the flowers from the sun. Ready to heal.

Rooster

Er er er. Er er er.

The rooster outside her window had been crowing for the last five minutes. No amount of covering her ears with her arms or burrowing into the light cotton blanket could muffle the piercing call to get up.

"Damn rooster," she muttered. "Wakin' up earlier and earlier the past three mornings." Denna rolled over and held back from yelling, "Quiet!" through the thin wooden plank walls of the cabin. No use waking anyone lucky enough to still be asleep.

Yesterday morning, the rooster had started with the early rays that came before the sun, and today there wasn't even any real light yet. Folks in the quarters were starting to get upset. Rooster reminded them of the overseer back in Carrol County, Kentucky that used to come around just as the sun came up and knock hard on the sides of cabins with the handle of his horsewhip. Some wondered what the whip would look like around his neck, but they left running instead of finding out; first through Indiana and then to Youngs' Prairie in southwestern Michigan where they stopped in the settlement that the Quakers had set up for them.

These white people weren't motivated by religious charity alone. Jones, Bonine, Bogue, and Shugart, they all wanted money from the moist land they bought, and needed workers to clear the trees from the prairie and the land around it. So, they offered escape and shelter to Negroes running from slavery. Men like Jones, who white people sometimes called "Nigger Bill" with affection, stole down to Kentucky twice a year at planting and harvesting time, hoping that negroes like Denna Casey, her husband William, Perry and Joe Sanford and seventy-five or so others would trade slavery in Kentucky for a little pay, some cabins, chickens and an account at Shugart's store.

Whether Denna wanted to stay or not, she still didn't know. No one really knew, because no one put much credence in the whole idea of staying in one place. The real questions were more like, how long?

What else? Is it safe? And, what part of freedom is this?

Living together on this land with other folks from where she'd been livin' made Denna feel some of those safe feelings she had hoped would come after a two-month trip by foot and sometimes cart North. Safety and freedom though, like a glued together bowl, was all a matter of how you turned the bowl. Some places you could see the crack and others you couldn't—but fact was, the bowl was always cracked just like they were never really safe or free. These plantation men from the South who called themselves master, refused to be beat by runaway Negroes and kept holding on to the idea that they could own anything they thought they could control. So they searched. Some traveled on trails throughout Michigan, Indiana, and Ohio for years. And since everyone like Joe, William, and her had lived in the hungry innards of control, they always kept an ear open for any rumbling of raiders and runners in Michigan and Indiana.

And now, that used-to-be-cute chick had come of age and started wakin' up folks earlier and earlier in the morning. "Rooster" as she had started calling him, was reminding her more and more of the overseer. He was different, but both seemed set on wanting to beat the sun each morning. Kept rushing daylight and work. William and Perry were starting to look long at Rooster—commenting on how much they needed them a chicken dinner to help get through all the work that Bonine wanted. Yep, Denna thought chicken was sounding good for supper too.

Only Rooster and a hen were left from the last brood, and his mother was long gone. Denna hadn't taken much pleasure in the chicken dinners that were Rooster's sisters and brothers. She ate them cause there wasn't much else to keep her going. Peanuts, the way she learned to make them from a woman from further South somewhere— Florida, she thought—were nowhere to be found up here. Not the kind she liked; the big boilin' kind that you could season with anything you wanted. The woman who taught her to make them—what did she call herself—Muja, she thought, told Denna that most people back where she lived—maybe it was Alabama—put hog meat in their peanuts.

"You don't need it, though," Muja told her. "If you can get some salt, that's all your tongue got to have to get what your body needs. Colored people eat too much hog anyway."

They all ate too many animals, Denna thought. They never had meat for every meal in Kentucky. Mostly they ate a lot of corn and sorghum molasses. When they did have meat though, they were always trying to stretch what little that man who was trying to call himself "Master" gave them or let them grow. But now, up here in the North, since they could eat more meat, seemed like that's all they wanted to do. They had already eaten the mother and all of her brood but Rooster and a hen.

Rooster never had been like the rest of the chicks. His brothers and sisters were constantly in people's doins'. Always lookin' for somethin' to eat and gettin' mad when nobody had anything for 'em. Joe and them ate the next to last hen from the brood the night before last after she ran peckin' after Joe when he came out with a piece of cornbread and didn't give her any.

Joe was cross that day 'cause there was also some lost huntin' dog, kind of blue, black, red and white, that came around that morning. The dog was so skinny, her ribs poked out under her skin. Denna's first mind told her to give the dog something. She saw the dog sniff and glance toward Denna with her nose close to the ground, wondering if she was gonna get run off before she got a little something.

As Denna moved toward the cabin to see what they might have to spare, Joe shooed the dog away.

Looks too much like Gabe Sanford's blue tick, she thought. *Jus' like 'im, 'ceptin she littler, redder and skinnier.* "Git!" *Can't stand seeing anything that reminds me of that man and dogs.*

After the dog darted out of Joe's way, she glanced and sniffed again toward Denna and ran off.

They killed the hen the next day. Why somebody would want to eat something that was just as hungry as them and turned mean, Denna couldn't figure. Seemed like the hunger, the mean, or both would just get stuck in 'em somehow. Something not right about eatin' a body you didn't like.

But Rooster was different. He was shy and always hidin' from trouble. Rooster kind of sat back and waited to see how Joe or the others handled the rest before he approached them for food. If folks acted stingy or irritable, he just kinda made his way around Denna and William's cabin and pecked at what seemed like nothing—like he was making do with some trace of something that used to be there. For about three months now, Denna noticed Rooster pecking at the ground around their cabin and began tossing him a scrap here and there behind the cabin. She didn't know if she liked him for his unwillingness to fight or not. But until now, it was what had been saving his life. Still, for her and Rooster's sake, she wished he would quit with that crowing.

Er er er! Rooster called out, seemed like louder, more urgent than before.

Denna bolted from her pallet and went to the window. Rooster sat perched on top of an overturned bucket about three long steps from the window.

"Quiet, man," she half-whispered across to the rooster.

Er er er!

She didn't want to, in fact, shouldn't go out. It was still cold and dark, and she didn't want folks knowing she slept in William's nightshirt. She looked around the cabin for something to throw at Rooster and saw the bucket of corn kernels she was saving to grind.

Too dark, even if I could aim that good.

"Chicken for supper tonight," William groaned as he shifted in the bed and faced the wall.

Denna took a deep breath. "Nobody's killin' Rooster today. 'Cept maybe me." Clapping her hands hard and loud, she hush-yelled, "Go on, git. Got people talkin' about eatin' another chicken supper and you the only one left right now. You better find somethin' else to do besides wakin' up folks and makin' 'em mean in the mornin. Git."

"Must be four in the morning. Don't know why you tryin' to protect that rooster." William turned again, this time facing the window. "That's why my daddy said don't ever make no pet out of something to be 'et."

"We got plenty of food with all this corn we been pickin'."

"Yeah, but hot water cornbread ain't helpin' me sleep this morning or last."

"I don't know why he keeps gittin' up so early."

"Spiteful. Figure's he can't sleep; might as well have company."

During a fitful sleep the next night, Denna waited for Rooster and planned ways to quiet him. As night ended and a glow penetrated the tiniest edge of darkness, she woke with a start. At the exact moment she said to herself, *bout time for Rooster*, he cried out *Er er...* but before she could finish, *Yep, there he goes*, she heard his cry raise a pitch and stop.

She leapt to the floor and ran toward the window. "Perry Sanford, don't you mess with my rooster."

Through the window, she saw a figure of a man, fully dressed with a gun—a white man—lumber from Rooster's perching spot and toward Perry and Joe's cabin. She looked for Rooster in the shadows, her whole being darting with her eyes from cabin corners, to buckets, between Joe and Charles' cabins. Across to Miss Mary's to Miss Mary's cousin's. To the tree. The tree. There was Rooster running. Running away from the tree. Running back toward the cabin. Running, looking for his head.

In a blur, she recognized Gabe Sanford, the son from the plantation, pounding on Joe and Perry's door, calling them from out of their cabin. She saw Perry slip out the side window and run West—heard someone rap on her and William's door.

"Come out of there, William! Come on out Denna!"

She heard the first crack of the wooden door and moved out of the way as they crashed through it. She saw the eyes of the white man who meant to take them back, wildly focusing, greenish-brown, hard, and prepared to look at death.

Shotgun in one hand and a dog lead in the other, he snarled. "Come on now, William put down that stool!"

There was William with the three-legged stool. She saw him slam it upside Gabe Sanford's head, and she saw Gabe Sanford fall out cold on the floor. Another man from behind Sanford pinned William in his downswing, knocked away William's stool, and was wrestling him to the ground.

A bolt shot from Denna's spine to her eyes, and she saw the clear dark outline of the door against the building glow of morning. The only block to the opening was a confused dog bent over Sanford nuzzling and licking his face as the man lay still on the floor. She leaped over the dog and ran.

Pulsating shadows with guns and strings of hair popped out of the ground. One jerked his head in her direction—saw her, exchanged a few words with the other hunter who had Joe, and dashed toward her. She ducked and wove between cabins. Running.

The cornfield. The cornfield. A brief image of the cornfield began to pulse and pace her running as she sidestepped a tree, the edges of cabins, and ducked underneath clotheslines. *The cornfield. The cornfield. The cornfield. The cornfield. The cornfield. The cornfield.*

A bark.

The cornfield, the cornfield.

A bark. A bark.

The cornfield. Cornfield.

Bark.

She ran.

The stalks stood as a band of darkness in front of her. *The cornfield. The cornfield. Dive.* She dove into the field without bending a stalk.

"Howwwl!" the dog called out.

She was treed. *More distance. I gotta fight. More distance.* She kept running. Down one row, over two. She pivoted slightly in the air as she sliced through the stalks, blocked her face from the sharp edges of corn leaves. Back three again. Running.

The dog crashed through the field. "Howww!"

Turn, be still, and stand ready. Her body followed her mind and she stopped and lightened darkness with her eyes as she turned on her axis, sunk in her legs, and cocked her fists. "Poor dog, might have just lost someone you really care about and you about to get knocked out just like 'im," she whispered.

With no doubt that she would knock the mess out of that dog and no doubt that she was going anywhere near slavery, she ceased to fear teeth or claws and became them. *I'm not goin' back.*

"Howwwl!"

Dog sounds came closer. Maybe just two over. A hound's head darkened the ground about six stalks away and then she saw its form, head down, finding its way through the stalks. She was not going back. She heard the dog's quick breaths gathering her scent and sunk a little lower, right fist back, left hand ready to clench the dog's throat.

Two stalks away, it stopped and slowly lifted its eyes from the ground and saw her track.

Bigger. Ready to fight, teeth, claws. They both growled.

"Howwl...."

It stopped. *Rooster. Rooster running headless around the quarters. William and Sanders on the floor. The dog from the other day. Littler, skinnier. Sanford's dog. Been watching them. Sent the dog.*

This dog. Knew her scent from before. Spy dog. Had an advantage.

Neither moved. Denna stared into the eyes of the crouching dog; both of their teeth bared and feet dug into the ground. The dog just too skinny and the hunger feeding her meanness. The dog sniffed again, let out a quiet, what seemed obligatory "Howwl!" and Denna knew the dog didn't want to fight. Knew she was a tracker, not a fighter. Knew even though Sanders couldn't have been treating her right, she would rather know if Sanders was all right than risk her own throat. For a moment, she saw the dog's eyes soften with something.

Sadness. Recall. Tired.

They growled.

Past the edge of the cornfield on the outside, they heard a whistle. The dog's ears lifted.

"Jackson!" a voice called. Not Sanders' voice. "Jackson!"

The dog lifted one ear, relaxed, then stiffened. Relaxed, then stiffened. Denna felt her bewilderment; saw the dog wondering if she should go to the voice if it wasn't Sanders calling.

"Jackson!"

Denna growled again.

"Jackson!" The voice started getting closer and Jackson quickly turned, sniffed around for its own scent, and shimmied the opposite direction of the voice through the cornfield. The muscles in Denna's shoulders, back, and fists relaxed; some with her breath, but she quickly strengthened her stance as the tracker approached, now just a few rows over in the direction that Jackson had just gone.

While Jackson had revealed Denna's presence through the intake of breath, the tracker crashed through the field, intentionally, haphazardly, breaking stalks. "Godam' niggers! Fucking cornfield! Just wait, wench! Just wait!"

As soon as she heard a pause in the tracker's stride and could discern that he was very near, Denna raised her leg and loudly cracked two cornstalks in front of her, leaving two standing as a shield between the two she just knocked down. She turned behind her and knocked down two more. She pivoted in the opening, widened her stance, put her left foot forward, sunk her weight into the ground again, and raised her fists at the height of her breasts. *Come on. Let's dance cracker. Come on over here.*

The sound was just enough to make the tracker think he had her, was close up on her. "Got you bitch!"

At the same moment, he pushed by the stalk next to Denna's first opening. Before he even knew he was that close, Denna, her mother, father, grandmother, grandfather, auntie, and her unborn children, shot out of Denna's right fist, struck him in the head and knocked him into the space she had made on the ground.

As he collided with the soil, she glimpsed the rifle he held close to his chest. His body covered the gun and he lay with his shadowed face to the ground. She saw him struggle to regain his ability to make his body follow his mind's demand to get up.

Denna quickly sunk back into her legs and her mind sifted just like her mother's hands searched rice for rotten kernels. *Who is this? Don't matter. The gun. Gun. Forgot about guns. Running. Growling. Knockin' this man. Forgot about guns. Momma, what to do about that gun? Don't wait for him to get up again. Rooster. William.*

Lightning surged through her and the power that had knocked the man to the ground and faced the dog, raised her leg and kicked the man in his ribs. With her heel, she rolled him over in his place. Either the blow to his body or his awareness of his increasing vulnerability jarred his consciousness, as he appeared to gain focus of the woman standing over him. He gripped the gun tighter with the intent of raising it to Denna when she lifted her leg again and repeatedly tried to crush his fingers against the metal barrel. When he could finally hold on no more, she grabbed the gun near the trigger and cracked him hard across the jaw with the butt of the gun.

"That's for Rooster."

As his eyes rolled and slightly dimmed, she could see the name Rooster brought nothing to mind for him. *Don't even know if he's the one killed Rooster. Don't matter. He's one with 'em.*

She checked his body for any intent to get up, but for now, he was beaten. Another surge went through her, and this time, it pulsed through her body and landed in a flash of faint light directly on the man's right temple. She knew instantly that the light glowed on the spot that would kill him. She raised the butt and aimed for the light. As she brought the butt down into his head, the force reversed back behind her toward the field, and the energy of the death blow spun her around and instantly propelled her into a running gait, further into the cornfield.

Nigger wench! There's your 'Nigger wench'! We'll see when somebody finds your hateful self laying in this cornfield beat by a woman! Run! Run! Run!

After she had run even deeper into the cornfield, she stopped and listened for quiet. When she felt her heart slow down, she sat. Then as the early morning light seeped through the stalks, she lay down and slept.

VANESSA ANYANSO

Coming Home

My parents are happiest when talking about home. It doesn't matter if it's Mom simply talking about how Grandpa trusted her most out of her nine siblings to fetch the newspaper from the store down the street, or my dad inadvertently hinting at, and then quickly denying, his Lagos party boy days. They both have the same warm nostalgia in their eyes, filled with a longing for the country they had not seen in well over twenty years.

But for me, their daughter, this country where they settled is the only home I'd ever known. They hadn't even gifted me the knowledge of their native language. They insisted on only speaking to me in English, so I had to settle for overheard phone conversations with family members back home or private chats among themselves. These stolen sentences had a rhythm filled with words that were foreign, yet beautiful and comforting to me.

There was one day in eighth grade when I came home to the sound of my parents talking in the kitchen. I softly closed the door, bent down, and carefully untied each of my shoes, trying my best to delay the moment where I greet them and they inevitably stop conversing in their energetic mix of Agbor, Igbo, Yoruba, and Pidgin English. I stood by the entrance for a few minutes, soaking in the distantly familiar sounds of my parents' language. I eventually greeted them and told them about my day before heading up to my room to do homework.

That dinner, between huge handfuls of egusi soup and fufu, the question that had been eating away at me for years, spilled onto our dinner table.

"Why did you guys never speak your languages around me?"

"*Ahn?*" My mom was not expecting this question. "Why are you asking?"

A lifelong list of reasons rushed into my mind. Instead, I shrugged. "Just wondering."

She sucked the spicy soup off each finger as she thought about an answer. Finally, in accented American English, "You have no use for it here. Where could you use it?"

"I dunno. Talking with you guys?"

"Do your father and I not speak English?"

"No, yeah. Like yeah, you do but, like..." I sighed. "Like it would be nice to have that connection to...back home." Back home. Those words were strangers in my mouth. Words I had no right to use.

"Ifeoma," my dad said. "Your name is Igbo, *abi*?"

"Yes, Daddy."

"And your mother and I are Igbo, *abi*?"

"Yes, Daddy."

"And you are our daughter, *abi*?"

"Yes, Daddy."

"Then you are connected. You are Nigerian," he said with finality and went back to eating his food.

Technically, I guess Dad was right. But outside of their stories (and mom's delicious cooking), I felt no tangible connection to their country. In fact, each story made Nigeria feel more distant than familiar. While it was home to my parents, to me, it was a constant reminder of the ocean between us. As I got older and more appreciative of my parents, I wanted to learn more about Nigeria. The thought that it would never be home to me, hurt. But, it was my parents' home, and I wanted to learn more about them. I finally got my chance the summer after my second year at university, when a close friend of my father offered to host me for a few months.

And that is how I found myself crammed between Asha, the daughter of my dad's friend, and our provisions for the next week, as the driver weaved around many potholes, constantly jerking us in all directions.

The drive from Lagos to Agbor was five hours. Lagos is where Uncle Emeka (Dad's friend) lives. I had arrived in Nigeria three weeks before with Asha. Even though she has always lived in Nigeria, her and Uncle visited us in the States so frequently that we had practically grown up together. And since we were attending college in the same city, we had grown even closer. On the twelve-hour flight to Lagos, she had taught me some basic words and phrases in Pidgin English (*How you Dey*) and some Yoruba slang (*Wahala*). She instructed me on how to act, especially around my seniors, and reminded me that it was *imperative* that I curtsied whenever greeting an adult.

"Stick by me when we go out, and just do whatever I do," she reminded me as we were waiting to get off the plane.

I lightly hit her. "You're enjoying this role reversal too much."

She was only a year younger than me, but she was still my junior, and even throughout our close friendship, that boundary was always present. Our parents had tried getting her to call me "Sister Ifeoma," as was customary, but I had vehemently protested. But even without that formality, our relationship was clear. Until this trip.

"Eh?" She laughed. "Maybe. But I'm also helping you out." She handed me my carry-on from the overhead bin. "Also. When we go to some places, don't talk."

"Excuse you?"

"You look Igbo," she said, "but you don't sound it. Once they hear you're American, they'll take advantage of you."

Even though she had a British accent (the result of some years spent schooling in London), as we made our way through customs, she easily slipped into her native Nigerian accent. There was still a British tilt to it, but it was unmistakably Nigerian.

And I still sounded unmistakably American.

Even with the pressure of trying not to seem like an *akata*, I still found myself having loads of fun. Asha and I attended shows, went for morning runs on Banana Island (the newest reclaimed land), watched many Nigerian movies and "reality" TV over endless plates of chin-chin and suya, and wasted way too many hours stuck in Lagos traffic.

The car speed over a deep pothole and I was thrown back to the present day. And the back of Uncle's seat. I had taken advantage of the lawlessness of Nigerian roads and had not worn a seatbelt once since I got there.

Asha laughed at me. I rubbed my forehead and glared at her.

"Ifeoma."

"Yes, Uncle?"

He tapped the window, drawing my attention to lush green. "An hour that way is Benin City, the capital of Edo state." He paused. He always talked as if he was tired. "Your grandmother is from there.

Your father grew up in Lagos, but this is his mother's state, so this is his home. You are from here too."

I felt a pang in my chest. I don't know why. I'd never met Grandma. She died when I was three. But I still felt something.

Two hours of potholes and views of villages between lush scenery later, we arrived in Agbor.

When everyone had been telling me about heading out to the village, I was expecting a small town, like something you'd find in the American Heartland. That's not the case here. In Nigeria, it seems that anywhere that isn't Lagos or Abuja (the capital) or some other big city is referred to as a village. As the car made its way over a hill, I got my first view.

It was massive. The road we were traveling on extended beyond the end of my vision and was the only open space I could see. There were no skyscrapers, but on each side of the road, houses were crammed so tight that it seemed to be the only open space for miles. The orange dust, characteristic to the area, seemed to gently color my view of the village. I expected to feel claustrophobic as we drove. Instead, the village opened up a bit more. I could make out dusty side roads lined with wooden structures and schoolchildren in uniform eating mangos on their way home. The roads were tight and potholes abundant, but there was a loosely organized chaos in the way overstuffed cars sped and motorcycles holding five people weaved between them and around potholes, while avoiding the children at the edge of the road who were running around women getting their hair braided and men laughing and arguing in front of stores. I imagined my mom as one of the players in this scene. A little girl with a few hundred naira in her hand, proudly jumping over potholes on her way to pick up the daily newspaper for her father.

When we reached Uncle's house, I followed Asha to her grandmother's room so we could greet her.

Asha curtsied, hugged her grandmother, and spoke to her in a language I hadn't heard before. After a minute of this, she then introduced me.

"Ma, this is Uncle Chukuma's daughter."

Her grandmother's eyes lit up, she grabbed my hand, pulled me closer to her, and started talking to me in that language. I just blinked.

Asha laughed. "She thinks you speak Edo." She then turned to her grandmother and (presumably) told her in Edo that I didn't know it. Or any other language for that matter.

Her grandma held my hand tighter and looked into my eyes. "I love you, I love you, I love you." She said over and over while kissing my hand. She then started talking in Edo, although this time I did recognize a few Igbo words thrown in.

"She's saying," Asha translated, "that Uncle Chucks is her son. And you are her daughter."

I felt another pang in my chest.

That evening, I called my parents and told them about the ride over and how I had met Uncle's mother.

"She actually knew your grandmother," Dad told me.

"Oh...wow." I didn't know what else to say. For some reason, knowing that made me a bit sad. "Wait, did she know yours too, Mom? You're from here."

"Yes," Mom said. "But we were closer with Nkechi's family. We would all play together when we were younger." Auntie Nkechi, Uncle's wife, grew up in this village as well. Dad actually met Uncle in a northern state during his Youth Corp, but judging from Mama Emeka's reaction, Dad had spent lots of time in this village afterward.

I made a vaguely positive noise.

"Also, have you contacted your Uncle yet?"

While most of my parents' relatives were either in the States, London, or South Africa, Mom's youngest (and favorite) brother still lived in this village with his family. In the same house Mom grew up in. Before I left, Mom had given me the address of the house and Uncle Michael's phone number. He had told her that he was actually going to be in Edo state for work, but that I could swing by the house whenever. But it would still be polite to call and tell him that I had arrived in the village.

I told Mom that I hadn't called him yet, but I was planning to see if I could find the house tomorrow. Maybe I'd call him when I got there.

The next afternoon, Asha and I pestered one of the drivers to help us find it. 161 Lagos Asaba Road. That was actually the main road we had driven on when entering the city, so we had probably passed it without knowing it. However, this was not like the States where every building had a nice, shiny plate displaying its numbers. Only about a fifth had numbers, and even then, they were hard to discern from the car. The driver drove slowly as other cars and motorcycles with three or four people and the occasional infant bound to a mother's back weaved around us and the potholes at high speeds. After about ten minutes, I noticed a bank, and Mom had said that her house used to be across from one. We decided that was our best shot at the moment.

The driver pulled onto the side of the road in front of a red two-story concrete house lightly covered with the orange dust common to this state. Asha had informed me that most stores in Nigeria weren't built. Rather, they were old homes that people rented out and did business out of. And judging from the two women braiding another woman's hair to the left of the entrance of what looked like a convenience store, it seemed like that had happened here.

Asha opened her door and I went to scoot out, but she blocked me.

"Stay in the car," she said. "You don't want people to know you're American. What's Auntie's maiden name? I'll ask them."

"Okereke."

She closed the door and went inside the store to ask.

A minute later, Asha came out the store and motioned for me to come. I joined her and a young boy led us to the side of the building and opened a gate. He pointed to a small white house behind the main one. "In there."

Asha tipped the boy then we started walking toward the house. My heart was pounding.

"Hello," Asha called into the open house. "Are the Okereke's here?"

A man came to the door and looked at us. He was bald, but if it wasn't for the tired look that comes with age in his eyes, I would have thought he was only in his thirties. He looked at us, well, mainly me. I had a feeling I knew who he was, but I couldn't be sure, Mom had left all pictures of her family here. I'd only talked to a few of her siblings over the phone.

Asha and I curtsied. "Afternoon, sir," Asha spoke for me. "She's Chianguo's daughter and we were looking for—"

"Me," he interrupted, still looking at me. "Ify, I'm your Uncle."

Before I could stop myself, I had thrown my arms around him in a tight hug. He froze for a moment, surprised, but slowly returned the hug. I had talked to him for maybe a total of eight hours over the past twenty years of my life. Our conversations had never lasted more than a few minutes, just enough for a simple hello and a question or two about school before handing the phone back to Mom. But for some reason, seeing him for the first time, my mother's beloved brother, I felt immediately connected.

About thirty seconds later, I disentangled myself. "Sorry Uncle, I just wasn't expecting to see you here. Mom said you were in Edo state for work."

"I was," he said, "but I came back when I heard you were coming." He had a soft voice. Unlike the loud, booming voices that almost all of my uncles had. They always sounded like they were yelling.

I felt another pang in my chest. "Oh...wow. Thank you."

"No *wahala*. Your cousins will be back from school soon. I will show you around."

Asha excused herself and said she would pick me up at seven.

Uncle Michael showed me the backyard, filled with mango, orange, and pear trees. He pointed out another small house on the land and told me it was where my mother was born. It was no bigger than a shed. As he told me more about the property and memories of a childhood spent under fruit trees, I kept glancing back at the small house.

We made our way to the main house where Uncle bought me mango juice from the convenience store as I tried to picture the staircase that used to be here. He asked me about how I was finding Abgor as we walked up the stairs on the side of the house to the second balcony. I drank my mango juice as he told me more about my mother in her youth and the many hours they had spent sitting in this very spot playing card games while overlooking the village.

The pang in my chest turned into a squeeze. I tried imagining what this house must have been like in its prime when there were no rooms being rented out, and it was filled with my mom and Uncle Raphael and their seven siblings and the countless cousins that moved in and out as they grew up. Mom had told me so many stories that happened in this very house, and now I was here.

My chest felt tighter, so I drank some more mango juice.

Grandpa's old room and office were rented out to a law firm, but I still felt something while standing there. Maybe it was his blood within me rejoicing at the fact it was home. I felt tears start to well up. But I swallowed them back down.

Uncle led me to the back part of the house that wasn't rented out and showed me each room, telling me what it was used for both then and now. Each time we exited a room, I looked over to the little shed among the mango trees.

"And this one," he said, opening the final room, "is shared by my two youngest." Pause. "It was also your mother's room."

The tightness in my chest was unbearable. This was Mommy's room. I sat on the bed and gently rubbed the sheets. These obviously weren't the same ones my mom used, but still, it felt comfortable to do so.

Without this room, this village, this country, I wouldn't have been. That tiny shed behind a house in a village an ocean away was the first place on earth my mother touched. This was my first time here, but I was still a product of this place. I didn't know the language, but I was *from* here. I couldn't understand or explain it to anyone, let alone myself. But there was something, some part of me, that I never realized had felt this loneliness, that felt at peace. This was my home. I may be an American, but this *is* my home. With that realization, the tightness in my chest disappeared. The tears were still flowing though. Now *I* had a story to tell my parents.

"Ify...are you okay?" He gently sat down next to me.

"Yes, Uncle. I'm just...happy."

How to Find A Husband

His words were harsh.

"I can't be with you," he said, with steady words that never cracked under the pressure of her heartbreak. He abandoned her with callousness. There was coldness in her bones.

Zuri spent most nights since his departure under silk bed sheets. The sheets that carried his scent and his memories. She hid beneath her covers, inhaling a death that smelled like honey blossoms.

Then, the phone rang.

It was loud and piercing. Punching through the air like a steel fist. It was him. Although he never had a distinct ringtone, the phone rang with a comforting familiarity that she couldn't ignore. She chewed on her bottom lip as she took one more hit of blossom. It rang again. She sat up and watched the phone dance along the mahogany surface of her nightstand. A tired smile dangled off the side of her face. It rang again. Then, again. And again.

She rocked back and forth to the rhythm of the dance. There was a desperation to the ring. It implored her to take heed. Zuri mocked its intrusion with arrogance. Her smile widened a bit more as the phone rang a bit longer.

Then, it stopped.

The back and forth rock slowed its pace. The smile dangled a little less. Silence crept in with derision. She glanced over at the pair of men's size 12s thrown haphazardly across the wall in the corner.

Zuri placed her bare feet on the cold floor and, as if that act alone served as a panic button, the phone rang again. She couldn't take another chance. She snatched it up from the nightstand and answered.

"Hello."

The line was quiet. She swallowed the puddle of saliva in her mouth and exhaled, squeezed a fistful of blossom sheet, and then stood up. She paced with hard steps as her heartbeat raced.

"Hello," she said again. This time with more annoyance. "Are you planning on saying something?"

When she heard breathing, she rolled her shoulders back. "I'll speak. You come into my life. Make love to me the way you do and then leave. Just like that?" She cleared her throat. "Did our year together mean nothing? And don't—don't—don't tell me you don't love me because I can *feel* it when you kiss me back."

More silence and heavy breathing.

Zuri balled up her fists and anchored them by her sides. "You know what you are? A coward."

The breath on the other line shifted, frustrated. A rapid inhale and exhale that only empowered Zuri.

"You think you can call me and what? Come back into my life? No. Not without an explanation. A *real* explanation. One that—

"He's dead."

It was a woman's voice. A dirty voice with umber undertones.

She glanced at the caller ID. She recognized the number but certainly not the voice. "Who is this?"

The woman's voice paused, then sighed. "I'm his wife."

A one-two combo that made her knees buckle. Her knees hit the floor with a loud thud. Saltwater filtered into her eye sockets as her hands trembled.

With a crack in her voice, Zuri replied, "He's...*was*...married?"

"You're not getting it." The woman smacked her lips. "He's been dead for ten years."

Zuri narrowed her gaze. She pulled the phone from her ear and stared at the caller ID, this time with irritation. The woman's voice irked her with such vengeance that her knees began to throb. "Who is this?"

"I told you who I am."

"No, really? Why are you calling me from Jared's phone?" *Jared.* Zuri pronounced his name as if she was sounding it out. "Jared Kennedy."

"I'm Lola. Kennedy. Jared's wife."

Zuri rubbed the center of her forehead as she collapsed onto the bed. "Did you say he's been dead for ten years?"

"Yes."

Zuri chuckled. A haughty chuckle.

She glanced at the phone, questioning her own sanity for a moment.

She contemplated saying something. Toying with the woman. Humoring the poor woman's lunacy as she fettered her own. However, Jared's voice played in her mind. She felt the residue of his touch on her skin. His kiss on her shoulder blade. She was enraged. Heartbroken and teased like a forgotten toy. She hung up.

She clasped the phone in her hand until it dug into her palm. When it rang again, vibrated along her veins, she groaned. She answered.

"Look, I don't know who you are or why you think I'm the one to play with but—"

"I know how this sounds. Trust me, I..." Lola's words trailed off as she cursed beneath her breath. "I know I sound crazy—"

"You *are* crazy. Jared hasn't been dead for ten years. We were together two weeks ago."

"I know."

"You *know*? If you know, then..."

"I can prove it. Let me prove—"

"I'm not letting you do—look, if Jared wants to end things, then fine. You're his wife. I'm—" Zuri chortled to herself, amused at how foolish she allowed herself to be. "I'm the *mistress*. You don't have to go through all this to get me to—"

"Mama Betty's. That's your spot, right? He took you there for your first date."

"How'd you—"

"That was *our* spot, too."

Zuri took a deep breath, placing a hand over her chest and counting the tempo of her heartbeat as she closed her eyes.

"I'll be there in twenty minutes."

The line went dead.

Zuri wanted to throw the phone across the room. She pinched her elbow in the hope that she'd awaken from this peculiar nightmare. However, as she stood there with sore knees and a tender elbow, she swallowed the second puddle of saliva in her mouth.

She didn't feel Jared's arms around her waist or his kiss on her skin anymore. At that moment, she felt alone. Lost and without purpose.

So, she put on a pair of size 12 work boots.

They sat across from each other in a quiet, rundown shack in Midtown. Zuri studied the woman as Lola stirred her spoon in a large cup of hot cocoa. Despite the heavy bags encasing her eyes and lines strewn about her face like cobwebs, Lola was an attractive woman. Nevertheless, life had been hard on her. It bent her back forward and drooped her lips into a permanent grimace.

Zuri cleared her throat and tucked a loose braid behind her ear as she leaned forward. "You plan on speaking any time soon?"

Lola raised her index finger but didn't look up. She brought her hot cocoa to her thin lips and blew. Her vacant eyes fluttered with satisfaction as she exhaled. She took a sip. A long, wet sip that dripped down her throat and flowed down to her toes. She sighed as she set the cup down. She looked up at Zuri and took in her beauty. With plump lips and tawny skin the color of whiskey, Lola understood what Jared saw in her. There was a glow in Zuri's eyes that still appeared hopeful. A hope that left Lola's years ago.

"You sure you don't want to order anything?"

"What I want is answers." Zuri scanned the empty room. "Is Jared here? Am I a part of some sick bit you two do?"

"I told you—"

Zuri rolled her eyes. "I know what you told me, Layla."

"It's Lola." Lola leaned forward. "What's your name?"

Zuri ran her tongue along the front of her teeth and then dropped her shoulders. "Zuri."

"I'm hoping we can remain civilized, Zuri. It is *my* husband you're sleeping with after all."

"Your *dead* husband."

"When's the last time you two spoke?"

"Two weeks ago, when he broke up with me."

"Do you have any pictures with him?"

"I'm not one of those types of girls. I don't need photographs to make me feel—"

"So, no. No photographs?"

Zuri narrowed her gaze while clenching her teeth to keep from speaking.

"Have your family or friends ever met him?"

Zuri didn't reply.

"A year you two have been dating, right?"

"You don't have to go through all this. I know I've been played. I know."

"Yes. You've been played but, not in the way that you think."

Zuri scooted her chair back and then plunked her left foot on top of the table. "These are *his* work boots. He left them at my apartment last weekend. How do these boots fit into your *dead man* story?"

Lola clenched her fists as if squeezing invisible oranges.

Lola retrieved a folder from her oversized tote bag. She laid out several photos, newspaper clippings, and a death certificate assigned to a Jared Kennedy. Zuri glanced down at the documents.

Police photos showing a bloody and unresponsive body that resembled Jared's. Newspaper clippings describing the accident and subsequent death of local column writer Jared Kennedy, survived by his wife, Lola Kennedy. Zuri looked up at Lola, who was enjoying her cocoa.

"My husband, Jared Kennedy, died in a car accident ten years ago." Lola sighed. "He was in the car with another woman. Imagine my surprise."

Zuri scrutinized the documents, searching for discrepancies. After a brief moment of delusion, she pushed them away. "Is this a joke?"

"If it was, it's not a very good one. And to be honest, I didn't invite you here to make you believe what I know to be true. I invited you here because he's missing."

Zuri paused. Shortly after, she burst into laughter.

Lola sat back in her chair and sipped her cocoa.

"Are you insane? Is there a doctor I need to call on your behalf?"

"You're not the only one."

"Excuse me?"

"Jared is attached to me. That '*til death do us part* mumbo jumbo isn't real. Even in death, he haunts me." Lola gulped the last of her cocoa and then slammed the empty mug on the table. "He cheated on me throughout our marriage, and not even death is enough to slow him down."

"Stop." Heat coursed through Zuri in a wave as she rubbed circles on her temples. She tapped her foot in a nervous pace as she swallowed a puff of air. "Are you telling me..." Zuri let out a short giggle as she struggled to get out the words, "you're telling me that your late husband has come back from the dead and has been having affairs with other women? Your husband's been ghosting me *and* other women?"

"I'm telling you that I can feel when he's with someone else. Since he's been back, I feel him in ways I never did before. And I know you feel it, too. The way his touch lingers on your skin even after he's gone."

Zuri touched her shoulder blade. Lola smiled.

"His kisses felt softer, hugs felt warmer. Everything about him felt decisively tangible."

"That still doesn't explain—"

"But there was something different about you. When he was with the others, they all felt hollow. But you felt warm, like a warm breeze." Lola paused. "I stopped feeling it when he left."

"And what did *it* feel like?"

"Like a hit of morphine that tasted like honey blossoms."

In a wave, Zuri felt a flash of coldness slither betwixt her bones. She traced her fingers along her goosebumps and counted the hairs that stood up. She looked into Lola's eyes and recognized bitterness. A devious disregard for her well-being that spilled over into their presence.

Lola exhaled with a defiant air of relief. "He's back."

The empty shack suddenly felt emptier. The air was drier. A chill permeated Zuri's senses.

"Why did you bring me here?"

"You were right. Jared *does* love you. And, that love came with a warmth that left me fiending."

Darkness slunk its way up to them, enclosing them in a cocoon of madness. Zuri felt arms wrapping around her waist. She looked down at her feet and felt stripped of her bearings. "What's happening?"

"I needed another hit, Zuri."

The room blurred as Zuri narrowed her gaze. The space between her and Lola increased as a weight pulled her back into a mischievous embrace.

"He's yours now."

The sun was out. It crawled over Zuri's face as it brushed last night's sleep off her face. She opened her eyes and sniffed honey blossom scented silk sheets. As she lay there, she tried to rationalize the feeling of a man's arm cupped around her waist. It was a full minute before Zuri looked down and acknowledged the familiar touch.

"Jared," she whispered.

The mattress stirred. "Good morning, beautiful."

Zuri took a deep breath and stood up. She examined the barely dressed man with midnight skin and portly lips. "What are you doing here?"

Jared lifted his head and squinted. "Where else would I be?"

"With your wife."

Jared reached for Zuri, which prompted her to pull away.

"Why do I feel so cold?"

Jared watched Zuri catalog recent events in her mind. He smirked as she chewed on her bottom lip in an anxious fret. She raked her hands through her braids as she meandered toward the bedroom door. Jared sat up. As she peered into his eyes, there was a listlessness that saturated her entire being. It claimed her optimism.

Jared smiled as Zuri's eyes sparkled with a sudden realization.

"You're attached to me, now."

Heart Conjure

Conjure finds Sade first, but Sade is the one to find Delario.

The two start dating during the last week of the trip, alarming the chaperones, who double their evening rounds. Despite the extra scrutiny, Sade and Delario find creative ways to sneak in frenzied make out sessions; Venice's winter chills both their lips.

She likes that he wants his own mojo pouch, and that he's already familiar with the ancestors who talk to him in the quiet spaces between his thoughts.

Sade buys a stuffed bear from a gift shop and brings it to all the museums. Between sites, she has the bear practice its Italian on Delario, and he smiles and says its accent isn't bad. All three take selfies together.

Back in the States, Sade and Delario keep dating and start hooking up. Delario brings her flowers and doughnuts for her birthday and isn't afraid to say she's his girlfriend, even when the track team girls hang around him dropping hints.

She gifts Delario a baby blue bag she's made by hand, the drawstring a bright green. He fills it with dried apples and cinnamon. *Sweet, like you.* Her insides warm. He makes Sade a pouch of deep, velvety purple, and she puts the carcass of a dead beetle inside. *Everyone ends up this way*, she says. Delario just laughs.

***

Without planning it, they both end up at CSU East Bay. Sade studies art history. *Because it's beautiful.* Delario's getting a degree in statistics. *Because it's practical.*

They don't rent an apartment together, but for all intents and purposes, they share Sade's. Her roommate stops talking to them the third week of classes, and starts going to her parents' house on the weekends. When the roommate is around, she fumes silently and leaves dirty dishes in the sink on purpose. Neither Sade or Delario mind the dirty dishes much.

I made a love potion the first week I met you, he tells her shyly.

I made one for you too.

***

When Delario goes down on Sade, she gasps, not because of his skill, but in awe of her own body and its powerful response. She lifts a hand backward to anchor herself against the wall, even as her mind rises to watch from above.

You okay?

She nods, draws her emotions back into herself, contains her forces. A few minutes later is the sudden crest, and the slow ebb. He kisses her to sleep.

When she wakes up, he's looking at her and playing with her hair.

You're named after the singer?

Yeah. My grandma was all into "No Ordinary Love."

Your grandma named you.

Yeah. She did conjure too.

Sade.

What?

I just like saying it. Unique.

***

They get ice cream on Venice Beach's main drag, where the constant crush of people has Sade's brain swirling and her stomach clenched. Delario picks strawberry, and hovers behind her while she tries to decide on a flavor.

She can sense his impatience, which makes it harder to concentrate.

Just pick one babe. You like lime, right? Get the sorbet.

She shoves him, half rough, half playful, and selects chocolate mint.

He gives her a look, but then he smiles, and she sees his irritation slide away. Delario hates chocolate, so, as they walk onto the beach, she eats the entire cone without him taking a bite. The sand trickles between her toes with each step, calling to her, *sister, sister, sister welcome.*

They set out their towels and become eager again, grainy hands gripping and sliding down each other's bodies. Children make castles nearby and parents make faces. Delario edges fingers beneath the

92

stretched fabric of her bikini top. Sade hears waves sighing and roaring in one ear, his breath the soundtrack for the other.

***

Sade takes Delario to The Forum for an R&B show with nobody famous. She can tell he's a little bored at first, his eight-hour shift at the diner catching up with him. His eyelids droop, and he stifles a yawn.

They are both ambushed by delight when the second act is a blast, the artist coming down off the stage and into the audience right where they are sitting. Delario shakes the performer's hand.

Whoa, he says.

Soon after, a gleeful spirit takes over both of them at the same time, twirling their bodies, and mashing their limbs together. It's Delario's first time experiencing an outside energy riding him. The music becomes a carousel, and all they can do is hang on.

In the beginning, Delario's smile is genuine, easy and relaxed. Then his face develops an artificial grimace, like some threatened animal. He grinds his teeth and squeezes his eyes shut. *I couldn't turn it off,* he tells her later, accusation dripping from his voice. *I was trapped inside my own body.*

For her, the experience was the opposite. A spirit taking over sets her free.

***

Sade makes Delario a small bottle tree in apology. Even though the spirit at the concert wasn't a bad one, she thinks maybe it'll make him feel better to have protection. She scavenges recycling bins for a week, but only finds two vodka containers and one growler of the right color. Sade goes to the Dollar Tree, buys some cheap blue paint, and colors seven Corona bottles.

She pictures Delario as she twists scrap wire together for the branches. She speaks softly, as though he were there in the room with her, casting a spell to keep him nearer to the earthly world.

Though I walk through the valley...of the shadow of death...I will fear...no evil.

He takes the bottle tree, but doesn't say thank you.

***

Delario is the one to find the exhibit at the local history museum. "American Folk Magic in Modern Culture," says white lettering just outside the display hall. Sade stops to read the description below the bolded words, while Delario moves inside. One line sticks out to her. *Folk magic, also known colloquially as 'hoodoo,' or 'conjure' is increasingly embraced by young Black women as a means of reconnecting to their West African roots.*

Sade follows Delario's trail into the exhibit and finds hardly anyone around besides the docent, who has a curly beard and stands in the corner, face blank as marble. Her attention is immediately drawn to the painting at the center of the back wall, its surface pure gold. She walks over and reads the placard, which tells her that gold represents attraction. Attraction to wealth, yes, but also to spirits and other influential energies.

Except gold doesn't quite capture what she's seeing. The exact color is impossible to describe. Beach, earth, and sun. Burnt lemons, their zest, and a daffodil in evening richness. The gilt notes are an invitation, the warm oil pigment calling to Sade.

She closes the distance between her and the painting with a few steps and places her palm against the shine. Sade presses her fingertips to the tight weave, surprised to feel the heat of hesitant flames tickling her skin.

You can't touch that.

Delario's fingers around her wrist look disproportionately long and thin, almost obscene. He snatches her arm away.

You're so crazy.

Delario has said the words before, but always accompanied by a rueful smile and a shake of his head. This time, they have an edge, like he's trying to jostle her. He walks away before Sade can say anything back.

***

February finds Sade single and discombobulated, as though her parts are strewn about a too large room. The part of her heart where Delario had lived seems shredded and atrophied, the same as some animal left on the side of the road. She decides to take matters into her own hands.

Sade mixes aloe, barley, lavender, and rose. Sprinkles them into a small, tin basin of water in her lap. She's sitting in the tub, body nude as the new moon, as she pours the concoction over her head. Sade's eyes close of their own volition, and she allows the scents to wash down her face, dripping over her chin to land with a splash on the white porcelain.

Sade waits to feel different. She can't sense it yet, but she also knows the magic will settle. She'll feel it first as a tingling on her skin, and then as a vibration below the surface, like a million bees were buzzing there. Then the influence will meld itself to her flesh, becoming part of her very make up.

Sade can't tell how long the full process will take. It could be hours, days, or weeks. She knows no one who could illuminate the process for her. What Sade does know is that, over time, her bones will absorb this potion for fractures.

She pictures herself a wellspring of renewal, imagines the second when the light will shine from her and burst her old self to pieces. Sade feels a flutter shake her core. *I'll have a different magic then*, she thinks. *I'll be a different kind of free.*

The Prell Sisters of Alabama

Miss Emma Prell, the oldest of the sisters, taught me how to read literature and type. She was stern, perfectly dressed in corduroy jackets and skirts of blues, browns, and greens, always with a light-colored starched and ironed cotton blouse and gold cuff links. Her suede shoes always matched her outfits. In the spring, she wore pastel-colored shirtwaist dresses with matching pumps. She didn't smile much like Miss Ella, who was the prettiest of the Prell sisters. But Miss Emma pushed us to do better, "take notes as you read literature until you get used to the story." I learned to type 120 words per minute in her typing class. Another gift she gave me was diagraming sentences, which taught me to love words.

"And by all means, use the dictionary," she preached, as she paced around the classroom in our four-roomed segregated school next to the church it was named for. Bethel. We read *Animal House, The Scarlet Letter, The Catcher in the Rye, Macbeth,* and some Shakespeare plays. I'm sure I didn't understand the total literary meaning of those classics, but it was the beginning of my journey to critical thinking.

The summer I turned thirteen, I got my period and read *Gone With the Wind.* Pleased with myself that I had read such a big book, I told everybody; but I stopped when I figured out that most folks didn't know what I was talking about. Not only was it a big book, the dialogue was more difficult than reading the Bible. But Miss Emma Prell was very impressed. In fact, she sent me a handwritten letter in the mail. Her name and address were sprawled over the top of the baby blue stationery. The pretty paper sang a joyous song to my heart. I felt like we were members of a secret club of admiration. She congratulated me on such a marvelous accomplishment.

This was the beginning of me reading important books, she wrote. I read the perfectly written letter every night before I went to sleep. Afterward, I prayed that I would one day write as beautifully.

The third and youngest Prell sister, Miss Eleanor, taught my youngest sister at Shady Grove School. She loved to laugh, which showed off her sparkling personality. She sported a huge Afro and wore clothes made from African prints, since she had lived in Ghana for two years when she was in the Peace Corps. She looked like Angela Davis wearing Dashikis. At the beginning of the school year, she presented a program with a projector showing us her Ghana pictures. The children looked so pitiful and raggedy. None of them smiled. I guess they didn't have much to smile about. We understood what our parents meant when they told us, "Eat your food, children in Africa are starving." Miss Eleanor's main conversation was about power to the people. She called everybody "my sister" or "my brother."

Miss Ella, the prettiest of the sisters, got along with everybody; Mr. Knight, our principal, was the only person who had any trouble with her. She taught math and science. Mr. Knight's booming voice sounded more like that of a Baptist preacher than a school principal. He often used his voice to assure us we'd never amount to nothing. In fact, none of us would ever set foot outside of Barbour County unless it was to prison, he often added. He wore blue and brown slick and shiny looking suits, white shirts only with flowered matching ties. We heard he made his children shine his shoes before they went to bed every night. We thought his children also shined his bald head with a biscuit every morning before he came to school.

Katie Payne, one grade ahead of me, couldn't come back to school. She had to get married over the summer to Leroy Rumph. Everybody was talking about her pregnancy. My stomach cramped from my first period.

The next weekend I ran into Katie working at the Piggy Wiggly. I was happy to see her but didn't know what to say. I tried to act natural.

"Me and Leroy is gonna get married anyway."

"I know. How you feeling?"

She looked the same, but she was getting plump, and her hair was longer and thicker.

"Get sick in the mornings a lot, but that's easing up now. My feet swell from standing so much. Leroy soaks them in Epsom salt every night when he come home from working at the barbershop. He's real sweet."

I was glad when other customers lined up. "That's nice. I have to go, but I see you later. I miss you."

"I miss y'all too. Can't wait for you to come and see me."

We hugged.

"I will, soon."

That was the same summer that Big Mama told my sisters and me that when the ambulance came to the house to get dead Daisy, Little Mama ran behind it, and when she couldn't catch it, she rolled behind it like a log. She screamed so hard she lost her voice for a week. It took Mr. Gus Eustey (before he lost his leg) and two other men from the community to bring her home. Dr. Faircloth came and gave her a shot. Big Mama said she slept for two days.

The week before our Thanksgiving break, Miss Ella called a meeting with all the girls, fifth through seventh grades. Our Bethel School only went to the seventh grade. After the seventh grade, we rode the school bus about ten miles to attend the Barbour County Training School in Clayton, since there was no high school in Louisville for *us;* but there was a high school for white students. Miss Emma and Miss Eleanor seemed to show up out of nowhere for the meeting. We heard that Mr. Knight had told Miss Ella that she couldn't have *her* meeting on campus. She told him she could as long as she was conducting educational business. And what she was doing was called biology.

Quietly, the Prell sisters ushered us girls into the small and smelly auditorium like soldiers. No men were allowed. Miss Eleanor guarded the front door of the room. And Miss Emma stood at the back door.

I was nervous since I didn't know what to expect. My stomach ached even more. I bet Katie Payne's stomach hurt all the time with a baby growing in it like a balloon. Plus, her feet were swollen from working all day as a cashier at the Piggy Wiggly, and she had to get fatter. Having babies didn't sound like a good deal for girls. Leroy got to stay in school. All he had to do was work more hours at his uncle's barbershop.

Miss Emma spoke first. She talked about respect and responsibility that we owe to ourselves. "No one will respect you if you don't respect yourself." And it ended with the usual, "keep your skirt down and don't have sex until you're married, then you had to" that we heard from home, the church ladies, and other teachers. Afterward, we laughed, and I was able to relax some.

She passed out pamphlets called *Growing Up and Liking It*. I had never seen a book about how the female body works. We were told to wait until we take biology. I had just learned about periods last year, but not in detail. Just that our periods were something to fear because you bleed for about a week, and you could have a baby. Being a girl was complicated; there was so much to learn. She asked us if we knew what menstruation was. We all said yes, ma'am. That's good; first, we're going to dispel some of the myths and wise tales. We clapped and thanked her.

"Good afternoon my sisters, we're going to talk about the beautiful human body. There is not a more powerful gift from the universe than having the ability to bring life into the world. No one else can do that; it is to be honored," Miss Eleanor said.

All I could think was wow! She was the coolest and smartest person I've ever met; she wasn't just smart, but she was hip and cool. She sometimes called us Baby, and she used words like groovy, and everything was beautiful. I'd never met a hip person in Alabama. We took a 15-minute break to read the pamphlet in groups and come up with questions or comments. Miss Eleanor told us this was a safe space, and the more education and information we had about our lives, especially our bodies, the better decisions we'll make, which meant we'd be happier and productive human beings.

Unlike the other Prell sisters, Miss Eleanor was a student at Alabama State during the 1960s. "Family legacy be damn," is how the other sisters described her decision to go to Alabama State rather than Alabama A&M like other members of their family. But every year, the sisters put that difference aside and checked into the Tutwiler Hotel in downtown Birmingham to enjoy the Magic City Classic football game between Alabama State and Alabama A&M.

Miss Eleanor had been part of a protest at Alabama State in 1960 when more than a dozen students marched to the Montgomery County Courthouse. The students decided to sit-in to protest the segregated dining rooms at the courthouse. Policemen met them at the door with aimed guns and forced them to leave. The students were called niggers and were pushed outside by the police. Folks were taking their pictures. The pictures were sent to the governor and posted in the *Montgomery Advertiser*. The white folks of Montgomery demanded that the college be shut down since it was state-funded.

When we came back together, Miss Ella talked directly about Katie Payne.

"We should support Katie; I've already paid her a visit and will continue to do so. Hopefully, you'll reach out to her too. This is a time when a person needs their friends. What happened to her could happen to any of us if we're exposed. That's all I am able to say about that legally. But let me say this, please go to the clinic, it's free; see a doctor, a nurse, somebody if you need help in making major decisions in your life. And please, please, don't ever allow anyone to talk you into doing anything that is not in your best interest. You are our children with bright futures. Do you hear me?"

Miss Ella wiped her teary eyes. We knew she was serious. Our teachers didn't cry. After she composed herself, she finished her talk about good hygiene and how important it was to stay as clean as possible. Nothing I had heard about my period was true, except the cramping. Couldn't wash your hair, don't get caught in the rain, you could faint easily; wild animals might track you down since they smelled your blood.

"And if you ever need anything, we are right here without judgment," Miss Ella finished her talk. I felt more confident.

The next week a small cabinet was placed in the girl's coatroom with a note that said: *Please take whatever you need. This is your private space.* Inside the cabinets were sanitary napkins and belts, toothbrushes and toothpaste, washcloths, soap, and underwear.

Once a month, we held a full devotion. All eighty-something students and seven teachers gathered in the auditorium. Usually, somebody who could actually sing would sing at least one song, always a spiritual, sometimes two if it was a holiday. "Take My Hand" or "Down By the River Side" were the most common. Sometimes we'd have a special guest to talk to us about the value of education. At the end, we would repeat "The Lord's Prayer."

There didn't seem to be a special guest when Mr. Knight took the podium. I thought he was going to rant about how none of us Negroes would ever set foot out of Barbour County. Mr. Reed, our history teacher, told us it was his way of motivating us. Last year, when the smartest student in the whole school had to get married, he was fired up. "You see, I told you so."

I never understood why he thought rooting against us was motivation.

But on that day, Miss Ella and the other Prell sisters weren't having it. She stood up straight as a pine tree and started clapping in the middle of Mr. Knight's talk. Soon Miss Emma and Miss Eleanor joined her. Everybody was looking around in disbelief. I felt like I was participating in a civil rights protest, but not against evil white folks, but evil black folks.

Just when I thought I couldn't be shocked anymore, everybody was standing and clapping. After the Prell sisters, other women teachers followed, and then all of the teachers, which gave the students courage to stand.

By then, Mr. Knight had slipped out of the room. Miss Ella started singing, "All of God's Children Got Shoes."

Roses on the Wallpaper

From within the starchy tangle of her summer weight duvet, Precious yawned into reluctant wakefulness. A wispy grey circle formed by the shock of her warm breath against cold air signaled the January winter had finally invaded her tiny studio flat.

One eye lazily half-open, she stretched limbs already taut with a chilly numbness. Twisting around, she grabbed the thin cotton curtain hung loosely against the window behind her bed, grimacing at an overcast sky and droplets of ice that lined the inside of the glass pane. The dingy wallpaper opposite; rows of faded red roses with stumpy, thorn-infested green shoots assaulted her senses as it did every morning. Precious planned to redecorate as soon as she got a job and some decent money in her pocket, but for now, she counted the flowers line by line, hoping the monotony would lull her back to sleep well before she reached one hundred.

In her reveries of the night before, tropical black midnight was illuminated by the bright Jamaican moon, while the rhythmic swoosh of the waves beat time to her gentle lovemaking with Elian. She'd covered his face with kisses until the dream suddenly ended, leaving her with only a faint, sweet feeling of him holding her close.

The clattering of the letterbox propelled her out of bed, thoughts of sleep dispelled. Dragging a saggy jumper over her cotton nightie, she rushed barefoot into the hallway, dodging holes in the frayed grey carpet to retrieve her government check from a pile of recently delivered bills.

Leaning against the chipped Formica kitchen counter, she plugged in the kettle and tossed a tea bag into a cup, waiting but not hearing it begin to boil. The cold enamel against the back of her hand was a harsh reminder her electricity had run out the night before, and she'd have to refill the meter with fifty pence pieces to get basic amenities like heating and hot water.

In her bedroom, teeth chattering, she stripped naked and wiped herself clean with Johnson's Baby Wipes. She couldn't bear to wash in freezing water, so she sprayed on perfume, hoping the scent would cover the faint musty odor, which seeped from her pores and clung to her skin.

Precious pushed against the door of the library, to no avail. The strained handles of two plastic bags of shopping cut into the flesh on her fingers; brown bread, margarine, milk, eggs, two tins of baked beans, and three apples. She'd had to leave a box of pineapple juice at the till because she'd been caught out by Cost-Shop's inflated prices.

She tried again, but the only response was the dull creak of thick, unyielding wood. Normally the warmth of the hallway was a welcome greeting, but today with no entry and no shelter from the mid-winter winds, freezing raindrops landed on her neck and slid down her back one icy inch at a time.

On tiptoe, she peered through the windows of the Grade Two listed building. Librarians clutching mugs of steaming liquid exchanged languid comments ignoring the large wall clock, which clearly showed two minutes past nine. Precious checked the notice in the clear plastic box nailed to the outside wall: *Open Mon-Sat 9am to 6pm* it clearly stated. She dropped her bags and banged the door, hard.

Laurence, 'Community Librarian,' according to the blue and silver name badge pinned to his cardigan, frowned and pressed a concealed switch, remotely activating the sensors that opened the doors. A gust of frigid air swirled around the room, preceding Precious.

'Took your time,' she muttered, sided-eyeing the staff.

The scent of linen paper and new hard-backed books greeted her as she went straight to her usual PC at the furthest end of the row of monitors. It nestled in its own private alcove, unlike all of the others that faced into the main reading area. She logged on under the yellow-white fluorescent lights; happy she had this section of the library all to herself. Using her coat sleeve, she wiped sticky, disinfectant smelling fluid off the mouse, clicked swiftly past the 'I agree' legal statements, sure nobody ever read them, and typed *Yahoo Weather* into the browser. Soon the sun would rise over Jamaica, its rich, warm rays nudging Elian awake.

Yahoo flashed up a choice of locations across the island, from the famous hotel strip of Ocho Rios, to the cool climate and stunning greenery of the town of Mandeville and to the west, Montego Bay, the leisurely paced international resort. As usual, Precious ignored them in favor of the brash, capital city of Kingston, where Elian lived and worked.

Body odor wafted into the space around her as she pulled off her coat. She waved away the tangible reminder she hadn't washed properly and adjusted the thick white plastic headband that kept her hair from sticking out. The salon was too expensive, so she wore her hair natural, like a conscious sister. She scratched two tiny bumps on her ankle, brushing aside the idea of hundreds of nasty fleas flourishing in her bed-sit, focusing instead on the hope that she was in Elian's dreams.

Precious ran her tongue over her top lip, as she typed in her user name and her password, "doublepp" for Precious Powell. If Elian's name didn't flash up near the top of the list, he probably hadn't written, and she'd have to wait twenty-four endless hours before checking again.

She grinned like an idiot when his name surfaced. It was one of only three new emails in her inbox, sandwiched between junk ads for diet pills and Super Viagra. He'd stuck to his usual two and a half lines, a brief, but well-written communiqué full of warmth and humor, describing his collusion with his sister in throwing a surprise fiftieth birthday party for their dad. "Nuff hugs and back slapping!"

He hadn't described the setting, the music, or the food. He'd given no clue as to the guests or the presents, or whether or not they'd lit candles and sung Happy Birthday, but Precious didn't mind, after all, he'd written at 2 AM Jamaican time, probably assuming she'd fill in the blanks.

Coincidentally, she'd also recently had a surprise party for her twenty-fifth, she replied. Elian didn't need to know she honestly couldn't remember the last time any of her relatives had wished her Happy Birthday, and it had been a while since she'd seen thirty, let alone twenty-five. So rather than tell the depressing truth, she created whatever reality she thought he might like to hear.

The monitor flickered for a split second as a new, delayed message appeared from Elian. He'd written "My Fam!" in the subject line. Precious opened the attachment of a group photo; several men, women and teenagers, a bored cat, and a dog. Everybody, including the pets, wore party hats. Elian stood to the right of his dad. Precious appraised his long legs, low cut hair, dimpled cheek, and dark brown, captivating eyes, summing him up in two words: freaking gorgeous.

She pressed print, praying she'd find eighty pence somewhere in the bottom of her purse to pay for the color copy. She sent a bright note mentioning how happy everyone seemed and logged off.

At the counter, she fumbled in her bag, eventually finding two ten pence pieces and some loose copper coins. Laurence served her without making eye contact, until she asked if he had a spare plastic wallet. He looked at her with cold eyes, and she left before he could comment on how she'd almost vandalized his door.

Waiting in line at the bus stop, the pavement slippery with snow turned to sludge, she folded the photo in half and tucked it gently in-between the tins of baked beans and the loaf of brown bread, hugging the bag against her chest to shield it from the sleet now falling.

"Picture's a bit crinkled 'cos I've been carrying it around." Precious held it aloft.

Charlene shifted in her oversized settee, blinked at the photo of Elian and his family, then fixed her attention again on the TV news.

"Don't you think Elian looks like his dad?" Precious laid the picture on the table and smoothed out the creases. "How much would it cost to get it laminated?"

Charlene boosted the volume, rolling her eyes as Precious continued, her mouth full of curried mutton.

"He obviously likes me, else he wouldn't send personal stuff like this, would he?"

"Hm," Charlene wrinkled her brow. She pressed the remote, lowering the sound and calling up the subtitles, mostly a jumble of mistyped letters due to the operator's inability to keep up with the newsreader.

Precious swallowed her last mouthful. "You think it's all one-sided? It's not. If anything he's doing the giving and I'm—"

Charlene snapped the remote, switching off the tele. "He hasn't got a clue what you do, where you live, or even your surname."

"He does know my surname!"

"Your age?"

"He doesn't need to know everything!"

"Maybe when he realizes he's writing to an older chick, he'll find someone younger to play with. How old is he, mid-twenties?"

"He's a mature twenty-seven."

"He's a kid. If you think he's so grown, why are you lying to him?"

"I should tell him my last landlord illegally evicted me, stole my deposit, and now I'm on welfare and stuck in a dank, dingy flat till I can get my shit together? Yeah right."

"You're both living a fantasy."

Precious held up the picture. "Does he look like a liar?"

"No, but neither do you."

"Go back to your news, sorry I bothered you." Precious blinked away the hot wetness behind her eyes.

"Okay," Charlene held her hands up, contrite. "Girly chat about Elian. Stop crying, misery." She handed Precious a tissue. "First thing's first, how did you two meet?"

"He wrote an article online and it was really funny, cheered me up. I emailed him, told him how much I enjoyed it."

"And then what?"

"He emailed me back, or maybe I emailed him, dunno, but it kinda took off from there."

Throughout the bleak and freezing English winter, they'd written almost daily, apart from some Saturdays when the computers were always busy no matter how early Precious arrived and Sundays when the library was closed.

"Elian's an unusual name." Charlene inspected the picture.

"Combination of his mom and dad; Elizabeth and Juan."

"His dad's Spanish?"

"Dominican. He asks about my work sometimes, but I don't know what to say."

"You've got nothing to be ashamed of."

"He's a teacher. I didn't even make it to Uni, don't want him to think I'm dim."

"Probably got a wife in Kingston and a baby mother in the country, both urging him to find an English girl to suck dry. You'll end up supporting the lot of them if you're not careful."

"He's not married and he knows I'm not rich."

"We're all rich to them."

Precious was silent. She hated it when Charlene generalized.

"At least get someone to check him out. What's your cousin's name again, the one you write to?" Charlene persisted.

"Shelley-Anne? They don't live anywhere near each other. Jamaica's small, but it's not that small."

"What if he's no different from the others?"

"Don't say it: *you always fall too hard, Presh.*"

"Well, it's true!"

Precious closed her eyes, recalling the numerous times she'd cried on Charlene's shoulder. Sean's infidelity, two months into their brief and unhappy marriage. Troy's loose fists, a sudden shock after a year of living together. Joseph, a rebound relationship after which he'd stalked her.

"You can't compare Elian to them. He's intelligent and ambitious and we're on the same wavelength."

"You don't know what he's up to out there." Charlene cautioned.

"No one's gonna get hurt. Sticking to email is like safe sex; hygienic and environmentally friendly with no morning breath!"

Two weeks later the temperature plummeted, and despite wearing three layers of clothes, Precious shivered constantly in her moldy room. She changed her last £5 note into fifty pence pieces and emptied them into the meter. Now she had nothing left to buy food, and the draughty bed-sit was still cold. But most annoying was that without a bus pass, she couldn't get to the library to email Elian.

Charlene insisted Precious stay with her during the cold snap, but Precious demurred until the night the howling wind sent a startled rodent scurrying across her bed. At Charlene's house, they drank hot chocolate and ate cheese on toast, while Precious' story of her fight with the mouse made Charlene cry with laughter.

"I hate working in insurance!" Charlene slumped onto the chair and slipped off her shoes.

"Tough day?" Precious poured her a cup of herbal tea, sweetened with honey and spiced with cinnamon and nutmeg.

"Bad drivers whining on about other bad drivers! The accidents are never their fault!"

"If you hate it that much, leave."

"One of these days I'm gonna buy a house on a remote island, feel the sun on my face, wear skimpy clothes, and be at one with nature."

"Take me with you." Precious stirred the thick soup and opened the oven door to check the raisin loaf inside.

"I thought I could smell bread! You baked it? Wow!"

Over dinner, the women reminisced. As children, they'd lived three doors apart. Charlene's four-bedroom house had a conservatory, her family played Cluedo and ate supper. Precious lived five doors down in a two-bedroom maisonette with her mom and brother, they played Snakes and Ladders and ate dinner. Charlene's family was middle-class, Precious' family was working-class, but they went to the same school and were inseparable.

"Suppose I'd better get ready for another day in the fascinating world of accident claims." Charlene yawned and began to clear the table.

"I'll do that," Precious took the plates from her. 'I don't have to get up early in the morning."

"Except to check your emails."

"Yeah, the usual online search for jobs, leads, you know."

"He's still in contact?' Charlene's tone was light.

Precious ran the tap and filled the sink with soapy water.

"Still sending pictures? Still telling you all about himself, at least what he wants you to know?"

Precious stiffened. "It's not like that."

Charlene cut her off. "Let him miss you sometimes, Presh. Don't write for a few days, be enigmatic, men like that."

Precious creased her eyebrows. Playing games with Elian had never crossed her mind.

"Lovely dinner," Charlene called over her shoulder as she left the room, "what was in the soup?"

"Stuff I found in your fridge. Beef cuts, veggies, stock for flavor, little bit of garlic."

"Don't know why you're wasting your time chasing office work, it's obvious you should be a chef. G'nite."

The next day, Precious sat at the large oak table in Charlene's kitchen, cup of tea at her elbow, pile of chocolate digestives on a plate. She was supposed to be using Charlene's laptop to update her CV and send out speculative letters to employers, but so far had only checked her email.

Nothing but sleet and snow. Send some sunshine, nuh man! Precious re-read the last email she'd sent to Jamaica before reading Elian's new message.

"That's why I stay in the tropics. I couldn't last two seconds in the cold," he responded.

Hailstones slammed against the windows and hammered on the roof as Precious stretched her fingers over the keyboard. It was time. After all these weeks, she couldn't put it off any longer, she finally had to ask what her heart needed to know before she fell any further.

"Do you have a woman, El? A significant other? A pretty little thing who adores you?"

Shimmering bubbles floated in the sink, their rainbow colors obscuring the dirty dishes beneath them. Precious plunged her hands in, gasping at the prickly sensation of the hot water against her skin.

It was still nighttime in Kingston. She closed her eyes, picturing Elian in the place he'd known all his life. She prayed her heart would stay strong now she'd finally asked the unspoken question which had lingered between them since the beginning.

"I wondered when you'd ask!" was the opening line of Elian's reply.

Precious had had a restless night. Common sense told her he was bound to be seeing someone and anyway, for all he knew, maybe *she* was attached. Now that Charlene had finally left for work, grumbling about the inclement weather, *"Snowiest winter ever or what!"* Precious was free to focus all of her attention on her inbox.

"Ace columnist and three-time Kingston teacher of the year, aren't I a catch?" Even his boasts were endearing.

"What's she look like?" Precious pressed send.

"She's pretty like money, and we're about to get engaged." Surprisingly Elian was still online. "What did you expect from me, kid? Lonely life of a eunuch?"

Precious logged off without replying. She should have remained in blissful ignorance, but her foolish heart had pushed her too far. She'd taken a chance and now she was left with nothing.

She moved on automatic, separating delicate fabrics from woolens while snow fell steadily from grey, unyielding skies. She poured tea from the still-warm teapot and cupped it in her hands. Hot tears prickled her cheeks, growing cold by the time they splashed onto the table.

Precious had never relaxed in his arms, feeling safe and loved. She'd never felt the heat from his body as his lips touched hers, never even held his hand. Elian had never changed her flat tire or rescued her from a stranger's unwanted advances. He'd never pulled her close as she trembled during a horror film at the movies, wielded her trolley around a crowded supermarket on a Saturday morning, or watched a cheesy chick flick with her on a rainy Saturday night. He'd never surprised her with an unexpected lift home from work or rang her at midnight for a sexy booty call. He'd never bought flowers for her mom, watched cricket with her dad, or let himself in to feed her cat and water her plants while she was away.

They'd never lain awake at night in post-coital content. She'd never followed him around the house picking up his socks or nagging him about his clutter. She'd never fried plantain and ackee for his breakfast, seasoned saltfish and callaloo for his dinner, or even boiled water for his tea.

They'd never marveled at the syncopated rhythms of a jazz band playing live in the park. They'd never come across a new romantic restaurant, grown bored with an old one, discovered 'their song,' kissed in the rain, ordered a pizza, played Scrabble, loved their way through the Karma Sutra, avoided the in-laws, wandered aimlessly around the shops, or planned a life for their future babies and yet, despite the oceans which separated them and the life together they'd never have, she loved him.

Precious placed the folded piles of ironing on the kitchen table next to a large pot of stewed chicken and dumplings and a loaf of newly baked raisin bread. She scanned the room, checking everything was clean and tidy before sitting down with a pen and a piece of paper.

"Dear Charlene,"

Her note expressed gratitude for shelter from an uncompromising winter. She wanted to say something about the pain of unrequited love and how Charlene had been right, but the words wouldn't come, so instead, she wrote it was time she went home to count her roses.

"Lots of love,
P."

Several buses sped past, splashing her legs with dirty puddle water as her fingers and feet grew numb from the blistering cold. Precious shuffled amongst commuters in heavy overcoats and boots trying to convince herself there'd be a fiver in her purse to buy a few essentials at Cost-Shop.

Laurence heaved open the imposing door of the Library, but the ready confrontation in his eyes went unchallenged as Precious ignored him, her desire to check her emails dissipating like the dwindling winter sunshine.

Yo—Excuse Me, Miss

When she was nine years old, a man had followed her and her mother home from Bobby's Department store on Church Ave. She had noticed him inside of the store while she was trying to pick out a pair of jellies from a bin of women's shoes, thrown together in all sizes. She was flicking a shoe across the bin when she made eye contact with the man. She had looked away right as he was forming a smile. She did not know him. She kept looking for an 8½ pair and even considered hopping into the bin and flinging shoes left and right until she found them. She thought it was something that Lucy would do from *I Love Lucy*. Everyone would laugh at her as if she were smashing a bin filled with grapes. They would gather around her, grabbing the pairs that she didn't want. And when she finally found the correct pair and waved it into the camera, they'd carry her out on their shoulders.

But her purple and black-checkered skirt was too short for that kind of processional. She loved the skirt, but it was not a thing to play in. She looked up again and saw him making his way through the zigzag of bins filled with clothes and household supplies. She abandoned her hunt for shoes and walked toward the register, knowing her mother would be somewhere near there. She could feel the pressure of the crate under her young but full breasts; it's the way she had been leaning up against it. She crossed her arms, pouting and shielding her body, when she found her mother already paying the cashier. Her mother turned down and said, "Whastamatta with you? What I tell you about standing up straight." Her mother tugged on the bottom of her black spandex top to smooth out the gathered material at her chest. She shrugged her off as they walked out.

The walk home was about twenty blocks, and she kept looking back to be sure that he was following them. She would lock eyes with him and not return his smile. She would furrow her brows to let him know that she was on to him and was not afraid. She was not just any little girl. She was Altagracia "Grace" Charles. Daughter of Patricia Marie

Charles, who herself was the daughter of Ersulia "Sule" Charles in Port-au-Prince. The same Grandma Sule who dumped a bucket of piss and sputum on one of Patricia's teenaged admirers. That was to let him know to stop coming round the gate with his boleros. The same Patricia who fought off a rapist in the elevator of her first apartment building in New York City, by going for his eyeballs with her hands and kicking him in the balls like she had seen in American movies. But Patricia could not fight these men on her own for long, and so the spirits gave her Grace.

Grace's first fight was in kindergarten. She was a good kid who sang the Pledge of Allegiance at the top of her lungs and was the first to learn how to tie shoelaces using the wooden shoe frame and yarn laces in the corner of the classroom. She had fought a light-skinned boy named Tracy, who stopped coming to school quickly thereafter.

They had been playing tag in the yard, and Tracy was it. He had chased her and a few other girls into a frenzy. They had started running in a group, feeling safer in numbers but making them easier to corner in the back of the yard near one of the school exits. He had leaned over them as if deciding which one to curse with being 'it,' but loving their squeals and giggling faces. Grace was close to the front and, instead of tagging her, he had cupped the space right where the pleats in her jumper began. His fingers successfully hooked into the opening between her thighs, and he gave a devilish grin before unhanding her. The other girls, realizing that another game had started, ran off happy to escape Tracy.

Grace felt her face get hot against the Fall air, and it signaled her body to lash out. She flung her arm in his direction, but he dodged, and she missed. Her arm slicing through the air only gave her more momentum. He started to run from her backward, allowing her to see his dry lips cracking against his smile. She started running after that laughing head. He'd thought they were still playing. But she and the other girls knew otherwise. She ran and ran the expanse of the yard. He was starting to get tired and the other kids had already moved on to playing suicide and red light, green light, 1,2,3.

He dashed into the adjacent parking lot, an expansive lot that the Catholic school rented out to make more money. It was practically empty except for a few cars. They were not allowed to play there.

There was an imaginary line that indicated where the playground ended and the parking lot began. This was Tracy's way of signaling an
adult monitor to chase them and end the game. It was also a dare. He
hadn't thought that she would risk getting in trouble by the yard monitor, Sr. Corde. Grace had crossed the line without even hesitating.

When he saw her still coming, he darted to the furthest point, the
fence that blocked the lot from the pedestrians and traffic on Nostrand
Ave. He had leaned his back up against the gate and let his legs bend
forward a little. He looked defeated but still could not stop smiling.
She got ahold of him and, though out of breath, she pummeled him.
Her five-year-old fists aiming at the middle of his torso. His opened
jacket gave her direct contact with his sweatered belly. He threw a
hand to her face, but this only made her aim lower. She went for his
privates and said, "Don't touch me! EVER!" She didn't want to touch
him there. She did not want to touch anyone there, but he had left her
no choice.

Sister Corde had grabbed her by the back of her collar. She looked
up at the nun's grimacing face, and the judgment of her expression and
her pristine blue habit brought tears to her eyes.

"He touched me! He did it."

"What? Get yourselves together, will you. The both of youse!"

This signaled Tracy to get up from off the floor. He shot up and
dusted off his clothes.

"Did you not hear the bell? Get in your lines and stay outta this lot!"

Tracy released a smirk that only Grace thought she could see, as if
none of the punches had hurt him. He had sprinted toward the
schoolyard and his class.

"Now, stop crying you."

Grace wrapped one arm around Sr. Corde's waist as the nun rang
the bell one more time. She felt safe walking toward the others with
Sister by her side. As soon as they got back to the imaginary line, Sister
gave her a bump that disconnected their bodies. "Get in line and stop
playing with boys, okay?"

She had gotten in line but could feel that stupid Tracy still grinning
from his spot.

She did not tell her mother that this man was indeed following them.
He was not touching himself or making kissing faces like the others

she had seen staring at her on the city buses. He just kept smiling and occasionally winking. She was waiting for the right time to tell her mother. She did not want to alarm her without reason. How far would this guy go? Would he walk into their building? How bold was he?

They turned the corner to their street and, as they passed the only house on their block, Grace felt his gaze leave her. She turned over her right shoulder and saw him continue to walk toward Ocean Parkway. He turned one last time and she cut her eyes. *He might be back. He knows where we live now.*

Grace knew the story of her conception. How her mother had whimpered into a pillow while her birth father took advantage of a woman who was lost in a Brooklyn snowstorm. He had been a familiar face from back home. He had gotten too familiar with Patricia that night. She had succumbed, thinking it was her fault for not locking the door to his guest bedroom.

For a week after the incident, Grace left the house with her uncle's box cutter tucked in the band of her red and blue jumper. She feigned ignorance when he kept asking her and her mother for it. She kept telling him to check the creases in the couch where he slept.

II.

Living in his childhood bedroom, with Julissa and their newborn, Manny looked for any reason to leave the house. He would go get milk. He'd go pick up a can of tomato paste for his mom's stew chicken. He would go do the laundry for the two women and the baby. Anything that could let him breathe fresh air and not have to engage in an argument with Julissa. These errands were his only downtime. During the hour-long train ride to and from work, he'd be too busy gearing up for the grueling shift or winding down from it. At the restaurant, he was a Guy Friday. Initially hired to do inventory and stock, the owner took a liking to him and he practically replaced her assistant. Frederica was Italian and was an heiress to a pasta empire that was moving to New York City. At the first staff meeting, he could not help but stare at her breasts. The most beautiful, bountiful, middle-aged breasts he had ever seen in person. As she spoke about customer service and the Italian way, he watched her size 14 body jostle and bridle against a black wrap dress. He liked her instantly and wanted to please her. He never gave her direct eye contact; he thought dirty thoughts and didn't know how he could use his words otherwise.

While they were still working toward their soft opening at the restaurant, she had seen him counting takeout containers and put him on another task. She led with, "I'm sorry. But would you like to help me?" He had never heard a request like that. She had not ordered him to do something; she'd asked as if he had a choice. It was charming.

He dropped what he was doing and deferred to her in a way that would have made his boys laugh at him. Like, "How you pussy whipped from the smell alone, b?" He was embarrassed by their hypothetical thoughts.

From then on, in addition to his inventory tasks, he was to buy flowers in bulk, schedule their deliveries and prune them before they were strategically placed around the restaurant to look homely. When she needed fancy soap for the guest bathrooms from Anthropologie, she sent him with her credit card. When she needed someone to help order and move furniture into the temporary housing that they subsidized for the visiting Italian chefs, she sent him. He had even fixed a broken lock in her Chelsea apartment, a lavish two-bedroom that he'd heard the assistant remark had no personal touch. But Manny was impressed with the amount of space, with the fresh air, with the faint green walls. Yeah, she was away from her husband and her kids, but in here, she could just breathe after a long day. She had thanked him graciously when he'd fixed the lock to her walk-in closet. She had even offered him a glass of wine, signaling the end of his shift. He had smiled uncomfortably, almost sheepishly, and simply said, "No, thanks." He was trying to quickly pat down his pockets to assure he had his keys and cell phone when she offered to at least walk him out. She had leaned in and given him a customary kiss on the cheek.

"Buonanotte."

"Buena. noch"

"Buon-a-no-tte," she said again, locking eyes with him for emphasis.

"Buena notte," he said and smiled to make the moment less awkward, to apologize for not being able to grasp the difference after a month on the job.

"Practice, practice, practice!" She had pointed her index finger in the air playfully.

Once, she had been searching for a pair of blue Italian suede pumps that she swore were under her desk at the restaurant. She had sent her usual assistant, but he could not find them.

"Call Manny!" she had ordered in her Italian lilt.

Sure enough, he had asked for her apartment keys and found them in the corner of her walk-in closet—under a Hermes bag filled with headscarves that she had yet to unpack. If only he could take one for Julissa. She might complain less about his long hours and his long walks. If only he could use the beautiful silk patterns to stifle her endless nagging, he'd tie it over her mouth like a red bandana.

Julissa had not gone back to work since baby Leo was born. Now that the baby was three months old and Manny's mother starting assigning her cooking and cleaning tasks, Julissa claimed that job hunting was even harder than she'd remembered.

She had been working at a Duane Reade before the baby, and at five months, she decided that it was too much for one woman to bear. She had moved into his mom's apartment, a place he himself had been trying to leave. He had a part-time job at The Gap working overnight inventory and was going to school in the day for his commercial Driver's license. He loved the solitary nature of that job. If he worked his way high enough, he could drive across the country and spend nights in sterile, quiet hotels. He'd be gone most of the month, and his mom would appreciate the extra money. She might even cook him his favorite dishes on account of missing him while he was gone. She'd ask while placing maduros and escovitch fish before him, "And how was the trip this time?"

"Same old, same old." He'd sigh before digging into the sweet plantains and wrapping a pickled onion around his fork. But that was not how it worked out. He had gotten Julissa pregnant and had to stop school to get a full-time job to support his new addition.

Julissa was his Girl Friday. She was a part of the group of girls who would be invited to hang out in the lab. That's what his boys called it since they were teenagers because they thought it cool to be working on something down there. Freddy's father was a super of one of the buildings on East 21st, and so they had access to the basement downstairs. The basement was the size of the entire first floor, including all five apartments. They were however relegated to one section of the space because the smell of trash did not travel back there. Random egg crates still lined the wall as the lab used to be a recording studio. Their mixing material was still there, but now they used it to play music while they shared blunts and drank bottles of Ciroc. Freddy would always bring the girls, and they were just around to liven up the mood. After a while, a group of guys smoking and drinking had nothing better to do but to fall asleep in their chests and/or debate over whether Lebron was better than Jordan, Jay better than Nas, Kevin Hart better than Dave Chappelle. These seemingly lighthearted debates could easily lead to sparring matches and someone echoing while they left the confines of the lab, "You ain't shit, nigga! Word to me! You ain't shit."

If you asked him, he'd say that one thing led to another with Julissa. Manny had no real conception of how one became close to a woman. Beyond saying hello to women on the street when he was with his boys, he did not know how to really flirt or get their attention romantically. He did not remember that he had patted his side of the couch every time she came around. He did not remember draping his arm around her and offering her a sip from his cup. He only remembered tasting her green apple tongue and reaching for her butt to pull her closer.

III.

Grace was having a long week. This coming Sunday was the start of a busy season for the Catholic Archdiocese of New York. She was the executive assistant to the sprightly, silver-haired director. In anticipation of the holiday season, she was to help the director of Special Events with securing tables for the Advent Brunch that began the Sunday after Thanksgiving. It was a charity event, and everything from the invitations to securing the donations and guest list fell on Grace. She had spent most of that Friday in her modest heels, making last-minute runs to the post office for the director and putting the finishing touches on the venue. She did not want to come in on Saturday; she allowed herself at least one day a week to sleep in.

After adjusting the tablecloths at the venue, cutting away the strays along the bottoms of the crisp fabric, and getting facilities to replace the tables that wobbled, she called it a night. It was a little after 10pm when she headed to the 53rd Street M train. She loved this area at night. Usually crowded in the day with workers, shoppers, and tourists, Lexington Ave could be an intricate maze of crashing bodies. Especially in the colder months, people practically walked with their heads down and braced their shoulders for possible impact, knocking into each other, so accustomed to this motion that it felt as if they were merely brushing past each other. No hurt feelings, no "excuse me?" But at night, she had entire blocks to herself. She imagined living nearby in one of the doorman buildings. Close to work, close to her warm bed, close to the smiling face that opened the door for her and let her into the orange-scented lobby.

She found herself going over the Manhattan Bridge, her iPod playing a high-pitched pop song that she thought she had deleted. She sucked her teeth and quickly scanned for her more ambient sounds, nothing she could sing along to. More something she could fade into until she got to her stop in Flatbush. She noticed familiar bodies across from her, day workers leaning their heads against the rumbling train, some nodding off, some just happy that the day was over. She removed her headphones and figured she did not need to drown them out. This was a quiet train into Brooklyn filled with people burnt out from the week just like her.

Grace got off at Church Ave and remarked that the smell of piss was stronger than usual. Maybe there was rain in the air. She exited the station and fell into her rhythmic stride home. It was a fast walk, accented by her heels, and gave the impression that she had someplace to be and did not want to be stopped. She saw a guy coming toward her and became suddenly aware that she did not have her headphones in. This guy was going to say something to her. They always did in her neighborhood. But this time she could not act like she didn't hear him. It was too late to pull out her headphones. She was just going to walk past him, through him. She was bracing herself for the collision.

On his way from a drinking session at the lab, Manny spotted Grace walking with her usual hustle. He recognized her from the block but did not know her personally. He'd said hello to her a few times when he was with his boys leaning against the gated door to the lab. She never responded or even looked in their direction. She was impenetrable. He wanted to share a smile with her, something. Women like that enjoyed cups of coffee or glasses of wine after work. Past her furrowed brows and narrowed eyes, he could see she was a lady. She wore trench coats when it rained and taupe pea coats in the cold. Even in the summer, when most girls could be found wearing short shorts, she wore Bermudas and summer dresses. He knew she had a steady, good job. She was like clockwork. Up in the morning, back in the early evening, and running errands on the weekends. She was a busy lady and he just wanted to acknowledge that.

Pssssssssttt," he found himself hissing. He was trying to get her attention. Trying to lock eyes with her before they passed by each other. He even aligned his path a little closer to hers, and as he approached her, he said, "Evening sweetheart."

Instinctively, Grace sucked her teeth. She just knew he was going to say something. Manny felt that high-pitched sound grate against his nerves. How many times had Julissa sucked her teeth at him when he asked the simplest of questions; when he'd made the simplest of requests? He responded to Grace with the first words that came to him, "Shit, you ain't shit."

Grace swore he had whispered that word into her ear. Her ears were stinging as if someone had flicked it from behind. She felt threatened. She felt tried. She turned around and took a few paces toward him and rammed her front door key into the side of his ear. Manny stumbled to the side and initially thought he had been hit with a dull knife.

"What the fuck, bitch!" Manny grabbed his ear with both hands and fingered the inside, feeling the raw, burning skin of his canal.

"You, what the fuck! You, bitch!" Grace screamed while a few people leaving the bodega adjacent to the station watched. "Don't fucking talk to me; I don't know you!"

Manny had no words. He put his hands up as if he didn't want any trouble and just looked into her glassy eyes. She wagged her finger and said as if English wasn't her first language, "Don't—no more—talk to me."

He nodded but did not drop his gaze from hers.

A Day N' the Life

Big Sister's leg appeared between the drapes like a magic trick. Shiny and smooth, just like a Veet commercial. But Antoinette knew it wasn't no Veet that did that. She'd seen her shave those legs before, but right after drying them off with her Terry cloth towel, she'd grease them suckers up with raw shea butter. Antoinette didn't know when Big Sister started doing it, or why it always smelled like wet clay and flowers. Only reason she knew about clay was because Big Sister had her in all these white kid programs, 'cause basketball wasn't enough. Now she had pottery class on Tuesdays after school, gymnastics on Fridays, and basketball on Mondays and Wednesdays. Thinking on it, Antoinette did remember seeing Big Sister mix those chunks of shea butter with a clear oil, then she'd get the cake mixer. Those yellow bricks and oil would turn into fluffy cream like something they sold in those fancy smell good stores in the mall. She used it on them both every single day.

Antoinette quickly scribbled a few numbers down on the white notepad Big Sister bought her when she first moved in last summer. Mama let Big Sister take her, and no one ever spoke on it. The furry pink pen didn't match the pastel pink and fuchsia drapes that separated the hallway from the living room. It was hot pink—the one in the expensive box of markers.

"You done with them problems yet, Little Sister?"

"Why do you keep callin' me that, Fe—"

Big Sister unraveled her pointer finger from the shimmering stringed star beads hanging from the ceiling and pointed it at Antoinette. Antoinette's lips smacked together instantly. The popping sound clearly ricocheted off the white walls, filling the room with eight-year-old attitude.

"And why do I have to call you Big Sister all the time? That ain't your name! And mines definitely ain't *Little* Sister," she informed, making good and sure "little" had all the "ick" she could muster. Antoinette laid it on even thicker by scrunching her nose and poking out her bottom lip. A stank face that only a younger sibling could conjure up.

"First of all, fix your damn face. Secondly, ain't, *ain't* a word. It's isn't or is not. Annnd, *mine*, doesn't need an "s" on the end. See, that's why I got you doing these problems. Clearly, there's a lot you aren't learning at this new school. Let me see that notebook."

Antoinette's eyes rolled, and she smacked her lips again. Big Sister held her arm out as her weight shifted to her right leg, making her right hip poke out. Antoinette scooped the book up and extended her own arm into the air. She didn't bother to turn her head or move from her comfortable position sprawled out over the sea of giant patterned pillows that were once perfectly placed on the wooden floor. Moments passed as the spiral notebook dangled in her grasp, when she finally tossed a look over her shoulder. Big Sister still held her hand out with pink manicured nails. Done by her, of course, since she didn't believe in letting someone else do what she could do herself. Antoinette sighed loudly as she pried herself from the comfy pillows. Her four shoulder-length braids brushed over the straps of her purple tank top, and then rested on her bare skin. Her slender shoulders were just as shiny as Big Sister's legs, like a glazed donut, hold the white flakes.

"You really irk my last nerve, you know that?"

"I love you too, Little Sister. Now hurry it on up," Big Sister teased, with a smile that made her luscious lips sparkle more somehow. As if the generous amount of coconut oil wasn't enough. Especially against her moisturized Swiss Hot Chocolate skin.

Big Sister was a modern-day Sheba with proud 4C hair that she always slicked back into a ponytail. No one could tell if it was all hers or off the rack of Judy's Beauty Supply up the street from their old house. So they always, always asked to touch it. Her body was that of Hood Tales. Round C-cups that looked fye in any top, a small waist that fit perfectly in strong arms, and a video booty. Antoinette was the first to let people know Big Sister wasn't anybody's model or a gym rat. She ate like a rabbit but called it being a Vegan. And the worst part was, she tried to make her one too. Big Sister did yoga in the living room, or maybe it was Pilates. Been watching the Kardashians a little too much if you asked the younger.

Big Sister snatched the notepad out of Antoinette's hand the moment it touched her own.

"Rude," Antoinette chided.

"Mhmm." Big Sister brushed her off along with a wave of her free hand.

Antoinette went back to her colorful throne, the cushions silenced her dramatic plop.

"Unh unh. Now you had it right at first, but you gotta make sure you follow up after you find out what needs to be taken out. Look." Big Sister walked over to her baby sister and hunched over to be eye level.

Antoinette's eyes became that innocent kid round that made parents forget that their kid just bashed the screen of the new 72-inch they got with their income tax money.

For a brief moment, Antoinette saw her big sister. She saw the fifteen-year-old that would take her to the park district on Damen to play basketball, right before lunch on the weekend. She'd sit on top of the metal bench, her fresh white forces glistening in the sun. Shout out to her old toothbrush and the Christmas green can of powdered Clorox Mama always kept under the bathroom sink. Felicia made sure to wipe off the dirty seat before her shoes even touched it. Half hour or so would go by, and the dope dealers would pimp walk beside her, smelling like Black and Milds. They'd lick their Carmex medicated lips, and shoot their shot. Little did they know Felicia caught the 63 bus to the library twice a week. Once for learning and a second for pleasure. She knew all about the Hood Chronicles, and she wanted better than all that.

"Fe—Big Sister, how come you're like this now? Why'd you come out here with all these white folks?"

Big Sister gripped the notepad tighter before letting it fall to the floor. Her behind followed suit right after. "Who don't wanna live like white people?" she joked.

"Nah, forreal." Antoinette rolled her eyes.

"You got a real attitude problem, you know that? Anyway, fine. Cause I saw what they had, and I wanted in."

"And this is better than what you had before you left Mama?"

"Antoinette, you wildin', Joe. Don't talk about shit you know nothing about. What? You wanna go back to her passed out all day?

Forgetting to feed you? Needles on the table? You think kids should see shit like that?" Her chest heaved up and down, her bosom jiggled just slightly.

Antoinette chewed on her lip, while her gaze focused on the zig-zags hand-stitched on the pillow underneath her elbows. "No," she whispered like a child that had gotten in trouble but knew they weren't about to get spanked.

Antoinette wasn't no punk. A few cuss words weren't gonna make her flinch. She just hated it when anyone talked about Mama's problem. "But white people do it too! I seen it in the movies! What's so great about Rogers Park?"

Big Sister smiled. She knew her little sister missed the woman that birthed them. She gently flicked Antoinette right in the middle of the fivehead she always clowned her about.

"First of all, who you yellin' at? And secondly, you ain't got no business watching those kinds of movies. I'mma put a lock on my damn TV."

Antoinette swatted Big Sister's hand away from her face and followed up with an annoyed pout. "I thought ain't *wasn't* a word."

"Look, whatever. Just know you need to stay a kid for as long as possible. I had to grow up quick, and the shit wasn't fair. But it is what it is, and I'm okay with it. I gotta be the adult now. Which means I gotta teach you the way things should be taught. You ain't gotta learn how to survive on your own, and you damn sure don't have to struggle through life. That's why I came out here. So I hope you happy now."

The brown sisters stared at one another, silently coming to an understanding. Big Sister knew Antoinette was ahead of her years. She got a lot of things she shouldn't yet, or ever. But she was still her baby. And Big Sister would keep it that way for as long as she could. She'd prepare her for any and everything. Antoinette wouldn't be no weak bitch.

Big Sister flicked Little Sister again before picking the notebook back up.

"You're annoying, man!"

"Let's get these problems done so I can start dinner."

"Fine."

The setting sun beamed through the picture window several feet across from the lively drapes. Burnt orange and sparkling yellow hues cast a calming glow over the spacious room, illuminating the sisters' rich skin. After Big Sister explained the right steps to find out how much money needed to be saved from a check if she was supposed to be taking out thirty percent of the earnings, Antoinette snatched the furry pen from her hand.

"Rude," Big Sister said disapprovingly.

"Unh huh," Antoinette waved her off with her own manicured hand.

"Ooo chile. I told you to stop biting your nails!" Big Sister all but squealed like a pig at the Zoo, while examining the chipped purple polish.

"And I told you to stop tryin' to make me all girly like you. So I guess we both hard of hearing." Antoinette snapped her little skinny fingers, attitude and all.

"You are the biggest brat in life right now, I swear." Big Sister shook her head and got up from the floor. "Finish those problems and meet me in the kitchen. You gon' learn today!"

"Lame, I swear."

"What you said?"

"Nothin'. Deg."

"That's what I thought," Big Sister cheesed.

She wasn't Mama, that was plain as day. But she took care of Antoinette. She never forgot to feed her either.

Antoinette watched as Big Sister disappeared behind the curtains. The stringed beads flung against each other until they just swayed, and then stood still. Maybe one day Antoinette would be like Big Sister, hold the nail polish.

Donte's Choice

It was easy to catch the rhythm of moving packets, a steady stream until dawn. There would be a knock. Donte would slide open the wooden cutout in the door. Different fingers holding bills would come through the hole all night. Brown stubby fingers with rings of dirt under the nails, black long and tapered fingers, clean fingers with painted nails, and fat swollen fingers with no definition at all. Gee left fifty packets a night and would come back as the sky started to lighten. As Gee counted leftover packets and cash, Donte looked at his thick fingers with scars crisscrossing his knuckles as he peeled off bills to pay him. Gee always wore sunglasses, so it was hard to get a sense of his face without seeing his eyes. Donte could not tell if Gee suspected he was stealing or not.

Lloyd had hooked Donte up with Gee. Lloyd was his first friend. When Donte was four or five, his grandma let him on the front steps alone. Lloyd lived two doors down and was on his steps too. Their street was off a main avenue where a trolley ran, and row homes lined both sides of the street. Even though they were supposed to stay on the steps, they chased each other, playing hide and seek between the parked cars.

Now they would sit on the steps smoking cigarettes and sometimes sharing a forty-ounce. Lloyd had been selling for Gee for about three months and was sporting the new Jordans and a rope chain.

Donte was tired of bummin' cigarettes from Lloyd every time he wanted to smoke. He wanted to look fly with new sneakers and a fresh haircut. And then there was Derrick—his little brother. Derrick needed to look good for school, or he would be what Donte had been all throughout. Corny. In the fifth grade, he was teased for his "bobo" sneakers and high water pants. That was when his mom decided she would be a self-taught barber. She cut his hair at home, and it was always uneven. Mom-doo Don the boys had teased. He didn't want this

126

for Derrick. So, he asked Lloyd to get him in with Gee.

His mom used her welfare check on whatever she was into that month. When he was in seventh grade, it was a color thing. She started talking about how the right color could make you feel satisfied like a good meal, but the wrong color could choke the life out of you. She decided to paint the walls in their house that were dingy with kerosene smoke. Donte went with her to the hardware store and stood around while she looked through the color cards. Reds, blues, oranges, and greens. Her fingers picked card after card like she was picking flowers to smell. She held each card close to her face and closed her eyes. It seemed to Donte that she became something else for the moment. Later, as he opened the cans of orange, pink, and sky blue, Donte thought about how it might feel to jump into a color and be something else too. They painted test squares over the whole downstairs in one day, working around the clutter of partially refinished furniture, broken radios, and bolts of fabric that were relics of other projects.

After that day, they didn't paint anymore. His mother ran out of whatever it was that pushed her in the first place, and waited on the couch for next month's check.

By the time Donte stopped going to school, she had stopped finding new projects and settled on losing herself in the lights and colors of the casinos in Atlantic City.

At least when his grandma was alive, she was able to get the food stamps and some of the check before his mom used them up. But since she died, there was always an empty refrigerator. Derrick went to their aunt's house on most days to eat dinner, he ate free breakfast and lunch at school. But Donte wasn't in school anymore, and he felt too big to keep going to his aunt's house. He needed his own money.

"It's easy, man. Never mess up the money or the supply. You'll be straight," Lloyd said.

Donte thought it was something he could do, since he could count. There was a prick of knowing that he should find something else that didn't come with the danger of selling. A watercolor of feelings that ran together and turned into a brown mix he couldn't separate.

Donte had wanted to be a garbage man like his Uncle Ebbie. Uncle Ebbie would ride through the block holding on to the back of the truck. His body would bounce with the rhythm of the wheels. He would swing down, light like a dancer, and grab the cans in one move. Uncle Ebbie looked free and strong as he waved at Donte when the truck passed.

He realized later that being free and strong in the way Uncle Ebbie was would not be him. There was a test you had to take to work for the city. Donte could never make the letters in school stay in order on a page. Instead of looking at the mixed up letters, he would draw pictures of faces on his papers. Two years ago when he turned sixteen, he just stopped going to school altogether. The reading never came, but he still drew faces.

The first night, Lloyd met him and Gee on the corner next to a boarded-up storefront.

"Yo man, this is my boy Donte. I told you bout him—he's like fam," said Lloyd.

Gee had jail muscles—thick and built up. Donte felt his hand disappear when they shook and slapped in greeting. He felt Gee's eyes behind the sunglasses and felt even his bones were exposed like on an X-ray.

"Okay young boy, you ready?" Gee asked.

"Yeah man, I'm ready."

Gee unlocked a door on the side of the storefront. They went upstairs to the second-floor apartment. It was one big room with a stained mattress on the floor and smelled like the air on the subway steps. Urine mixed with warm staleness. Next to the mattress was a boom box and cassettes. A pile of old newspapers sat in a corner, next to empty forty bottles. From the one window in the room, you could see the avenue with cars and trolleys rolling by. The window had black metal bars across the bottom half.

There was a brown leather suitcase, worn with three buckles on the top, next to the mattress. Gee knelt down and opened the case. It contained small packs of cocaine rocks wrapped individually. Gee ran his hands through the packets that ran like beads through his thick fingers.

"This right here is my treasure. My heart," Gee said as his hands flexed and tightened around the suitcase. "You steal my treasure, you break my heart, and I break you. You got me, young boy?"

"Yeah, we good man," said Donte.

Some customers came back every night and sometimes several times in the same night. The night she came, Donte knew her by the look of her fingers. He would know Karimah's fingers anywhere, delicate with the thin black line on her ring fingernail. She held a crumpled ten-dollar bill. He covered her fingers with his hand as he took the money.

"Hey, is that you, Donte?"

Her voice, hoarse and light at the same time, brought him back to eighth grade at Douglas Middle School. Karimah Michaels. Donte's seat was behind hers in Mrs. Young's class. Kids were still calling him Mom-doo Don. Karimah had light brown eyes flecked with green and hair that made loose waves around her face. She was the color of peanut butter, and when the sunlight hit her hair, it turned reddish. Her fingers sometimes would brush his when she passed him papers, and he would feel his dick pulse. He would be glad he was sitting and no one could see.

She would turn around when she passed the papers back to him. Donte would cover whatever face he was drawing at the time. He felt Karimah would never see him because of what he didn't have. He was covered by static, like a bad picture on his TV.

Lloyd had told him not to talk to the crackheads that came through the night.

"They so slick man. The shit they come up with. Especially the girls. They be promising all kinds of pussy. Don't be dumb, just take the money and pass the packages."

But now it was Karimah. The girl he used to think about when he clutched himself in the dark imaging her hands instead of his own. He had long conversations with his mirror in the bathroom. Donte would get himself ready first, like she really would see him. Use Pink Lotion in his hair and brush it, trying to pretend it was freshly cut. He would check his nose for boogies and breathe into his hand, smelling his breath. Donte came up with all the things he would say to her.

"Did you hear the new one from Run DMC—Rock Box—that jawn is fresh," changing his expressions and his voice from his to hers. Now it was four years after eighth grade, and she said his name.

So he said, "Yeah, it's me."

"I thought I knew those hands. You sat behind me in school. Just so you know, I just smoke a little bit. I'm not gettin' high all the time."

Donte had heard she was a smoker. But he thought about her fingers touching his again like they had in eighth grade and didn't care. She came by a few nights a week. But she never asked for anything for free, and they would talk until the next customer came. Her voice slipped through the locked door.

Most nights, he listened to tapes and drew faces and fingers on the old newspapers in the room. Donte used the empty forty bottles if he had to pee. But sometimes he felt closed in. The walls would squeeze together, and the room shrank. He would get this built-up feeling in his chest that traveled up and closed his throat. He would turn up the sound on his mixtape, repeat the EPMD lyric *Boy you gots to chill* over and over again, just so he couldn't hear himself breathing hard. His fingers would feel numb, and he would look at his own hands. He had rounded nail beds and pudgy fingers, but the fingers would stretch and change, and he had the feeling his own fingers were choking him. The tingling would spread down his fingers to his arms. Donte wanted to break down the door when this happened and run down the avenue. But he couldn't get out of the room before Gee came.

He would walk around the edge of the room until he felt his fingers again, and his breathing slowed. Sometimes a knock on the door would save him from the paralyzing tingling. Whenever he opened the slot, he was hoping to see her fingers. The nights were shorter when she came by.

"You know where I stay, right?" Karimah said one night. "I want to see what you look like now. You should come by. I just be home babysitting my little sister."

He did know that he should not go, but also that he would. Donte waited, though, until she asked again.

Karimah lived on Kingsessing Street. The day he decided to go, it was like the first warm day after winter when you feel anything is possible. Her porch had baby walkers and strollers. He knocked on the door. The girl who answered was the Karimah he remembered, but not. It was as if he was in an alternate world where things are familiar but changed. Her hair was thin and short, with the edges thinned out, dull now in the sunlight. Karimah's eyes were larger and poked out from the leanness of her face. But when she took his hand and led him inside, she was the same girl from eighth grade again.

Furniture cluttered every part of the room, and it was dim. He almost didn't notice the little girl sleeping on the couch.

"Come on, let's go upstairs," she said.

He wondered if there was anyone else at home.

Karimah told him that she was going to Hair School in a couple of months. She was just waiting to save up enough from babysitting. Her mom was going to pay half if she could get the other half. She had a mannequin head that she had found and practiced hairstyles on. The head sat on the dresser with unblinking eyes, a witness in rollers.

Her room was filled with clothes and old toys. There was nowhere to sit but the bed. It was unmade, with sheets that looked like they used to be blue, now faded to grey.

"I'm going to smoke. You want to?"

He didn't want to, but he wanted to share something with her. He smelled the possibility of danger, but the pull of what he could have won out.

So he said, "Let's do it."

She filled the glass pipe and stuck the lighter flame underneath. Donte had tried cocaine before, but not crack. He and Lloyd had sniffed a couple of lines together. His heart had twisted and squeezed in his chest. In his mind, he had called out to God to save him because he knew he was dying. He promised God, in that desperate moment, he would never do cocaine again. He had thought of Len Bias and how he was dead now. But now here was Karimah with her fingers holding the pipe out to him like a lifeline.

As he inhaled, he felt he was drowning and being saved at the same time. She inhaled and blew the smoke in his face, and then she was kissing him and undoing his pants. He felt all the comforting weight of possibility as he released inside her. Afterward, she traced his face with her fingers, and he knew she could see him clearly.

After that, Donte went to her every day, and she came to him every night. They had a rhythm that they improvised together. It was their own song. He worked, looking forward to the days. Maybe this is what Uncle Ebbie felt like, swinging up and down on that truck.

Lloyd had asked him, "Man, you messin' with Karimah? I heard she be doin' dudes for money on the avenue. You better be careful 'cause Gee ain't playing."

"Man, you just jealous—she ain't like that. She don't need to be hustlin.'"

Donte had found a way of looking for rocks in the packets that were a little bigger and halving them so he would have an extra for her. He would carefully reseal the packets that he had opened.

The first time he did it, he was scared and started sweating when he heard the stairs creak with Gee's weight as he came up. Gee opened the door and went right to the suitcase like always. Donte thought he felt Gee's eyes linger on him when he paid him that morning. But he did everything the same.

When the extra rock or two that he gave her wasn't enough. He started leaving money when he left her house. More than he should have, but the idea of not leaving enough and seeing her in his mind on the avenue decided for him. But he was short of the money he had gotten used to. He started getting his haircut every other week instead of every week.

That last night Karimah came with no money.

"Hey Don, I'm short tonight. What you got for me?" Her voice touched the prism of color inside him.

"K, I'm out too."

She placed her fingers through the slot. Fingers—his with hers—twined. Then she pulled back. He felt that squeezing sensation around his neck.

"Hey K, hold up." Then he slid a bag through the slot.

"Thanks, Don. You my man."

He gave her the packet for nothing. The count would be short.

As the sky faded to grey from blue-black, Donte waited for Gee by the window. He thought about the mouse he found one day in the kitchen. Its back two legs were crushed in the metal bar of the trap. The mouse tried to free itself by twisting its body back and forth. Donte had picked up the trap and threw it out the back door into the alley. Maybe he should have opened the trap and let it free. It could have crawled away and found someplace it wanted to die instead of dying still trapped. But he only thought that now.

He heard Gee on the stairs. Each step sounded heavier as Gee got closer to the top. He came in and opened the suitcase. Donte looked through the bars of the window as Gee counted. When he finally looked at Gee, his sunglasses were off. The whites of his eyes were threaded with so many blood vessels that his eyes looked all red with a black center, and his lower lids were filled with pus.

"Nigga, you think I didn't know you been skimmin' for weeks? I wanted to see how much you'd try. Now you just taking whole packets."

"Hold up, man, let me tell you," Donte said, as he backed against the window.

Gee's grabbed Donte's neck with his thick fingers and squeezed. Gee's face was so close that Donte could only look at his eyes. He started to see colors in the pus as he struggled and lost his air. He felt the edges of color pulling him into blackness. He saw flashes of faces— all the ones he'd drawn, and he wondered if Karimah's fingers would tremble when she heard.

Congratulations, It's A Girl

Tahani stood at her dresser mirror, trying to coax her massive sandy blond hair into a bun. The curls resisted the pins she used to hold them down, slipping out and springing back to life around her hairline. They weren't used to being tamed; she fed their desire for freedom with coconut oil-dipped fingers and silky hair puddings that brought them to their full glory. But not today. Today she needed them to behave.

She wore a mauve-colored jersey dress with bell sleeves accented in off-white lace. The stretchy fabric was a mistake; she already knew. Her mother's eyes, hazel like her own, would sharpen at the sight of her daughter's curves. The lace headscarf draped loosely over her head wouldn't help either.

Normally, getting dressed and styling her hair was the highlight of Tahani's day. Twenty-three years old, she reserved a girlish delight for primping. But she was getting ready to attend the wedding of the youngest of her six older brothers. Suad was the most tolerable of her brothers, but that wasn't saying much, and their overwhelming presence—all of them and their tiresome wives, disdaining her like her mother—filled her with dread.

Since leaving home at eighteen, she only saw her family at the masjid and community events. She avoided visits home. Her father was easy-going, eager to keep peace, but his gentle presence was overshadowed by her mother's disappointed silence and her brothers' stinging barbs. Her younger brother Hadi was the only family member with whom she kept close ties.

Her friend Fatima came into the room, Tahani's two daughters trailing behind her.

"Hi, Ummi," Aliyah, her five-year-old, said, hopping on white stockinged toes.

Safia, who would turn four soon, copied her sister. The girls perched on Tahani's bed like cake toppings, the skirts of their pale rose-colored tulle dresses billowing out around them. They wore matching one-piece hijabs with sequined headbands. Tahani had bought them for the girls to wear to the masjid, but they'd taken to the scarves so much they wore them almost every day.

"My beauties," Tahani cooed, kissing them on their foreheads.

She pinched gently at Safia's, then Aliyah's cheek. Their light brown skin glowed. Their plump arms too. Fatima must have rubbed them down with cocoa butter; they smelled faintly like cookies.

"Thanks for getting them ready."

"Of course," Fatima said.

She looked at Tahani's dress and pressed her lips together. Tahani raised an eyebrow at her friend.

"What?" Fatima asked, feigning innocence.

Tahani smirked in response. Fatima wore a slate gray empire waist dress with a lighter gray duster that reached past her knees. Fatima, who had run away to Atlanta five years ago after her fiancé died, had returned to New Orleans and got religious, wearing opaque headscarves that covered all of her neck and chest, and dresses over pants. She'd confessed to Tahani that she'd had a "friend" in Atlanta. "Past tense," she'd stressed. Tahani had only grinned. She'd had a friend too, and he'd stuck around only long enough to give her two babies.

Fatima stood next to Tahani at the mirror and patted her lips with tinted lip balm. "So," she said, drawing the word out, "I haven't seen Asaad in a while. Is he going to the wedding?"

Tahani flicked her eyes at Fatima in the mirror and didn't respond. She tossed random makeup items into her bag. "He asked me to marry him," she said in a muted voice.

Fatima squealed and turned to Tahani, her eyes giddy.

"I told him no," she said.

Fatima's shoulders dropped. "Why?" her voice as hurt as Asaad's had been.

Tahani shook her head. "He's twenty-two. I have two kids. I can't saddle him with my shit."

Fatima reached to touch her friend's shoulder, but Tahani shrank back. "I'll bring the girls down to the car."

Tahani winked at her daughters as they left then turned back to the mirror. She grabbed a black eye pencil and drew a thin line along each eyelid, smudging the end up into a tail, the way Asaad liked. "Tiger eyes," he called them, growling at her. She tossed the pencil down.

Now she was ready.

***

The wedding was at the Hilton by the riverfront. Tahani had called Hadi as soon as she received her invitation in the mail.

"A hotel?" she asked.

"Yuuup," Hadi laughed.

"Ummi let them?"

"Apparently Suad didn't give her much choice in the matter, said it's what Jameelah wanted. He's a kept man already."

All of their older brothers had been married at small ceremonies at a masjid. The only thing plentiful was the food to be distributed to the community. The Kabeer family didn't do lavish anything. *Humble yourselves in this world, or be humbled before your Lord.* Their mother's favorite saying whenever they wanted something name brand or brightly colored.

"I hear there'll be a band, too," Hadi had said.

"Shut up."

It was true. The faint tinkle of piano keys and the whine of a saxophone hit Tahani's ears as soon as the elevator doors opened to the third-floor ballroom. Leading her girls out of the elevator with Fatima trailing her, she tripped on the thick carpet.

"Damn, you wouldn't even hear the Hulk on these floors," she said, too loudly.

Hadi stood in the hall outside the entrance. He wore a black suit and tugged at the knot in his tie. Tahani smiled and waved.

"Uncle Hadi!" Aliyah squealed. She and Safia ran and tackled his legs.

"What's up, squirts?" he said, tickling them both under their chins.

Safia patted his coat pockets. "Peppermints?"

Hadi cocked his head at Tahani. "Man, they don't waste time, huh?" He gave them each a mint then leaned over them to hug his sister.

"Look at you looking all clean," Tahani said. "Let me check behind your ears." She went to pull at his ear, but he hopped out of her reach.

"Come on, man."

His cheeks flushed red behind his freckles. He adjusted the lapels of his coat and looked at Fatima. He waved shyly. Fatima smiled and turned to follow Aliyah and Safia into the ballroom. Tahani and Hadi sauntered in behind them.

Everything was cream and gold. Each table had a floral centerpiece of white lilies on a bed of gold tulle with little candles dotted around them. The chairs were covered in mint green satin with gold sashes tied in bows at the back. Chandeliers hung from the ceiling. The whole room was bathed in a rich honey glow.

"This lighting is incredible," Tahani said. "It even makes you look good."

"You got all the jokes," Hadi said. "I thought your boy was the co-median."

Tahani ignored the reference to Asaad. She touched the edges of her brother's golden hair, cut into a high top fade. "Seriously though, I see you with your fresh cut."

He'd worn his hair in a short afro as long as she could remember. Always too skinny, he was finally starting to fill out a little. His suit actually fit him. He tilted his chin up and stroked his measly facial hair with the back of his hand, then stopped suddenly and ducked his head.

"Heads up," he said.

"Ummi?" she whispered.

"The Beardy Bunch."

She turned to see four of her brothers approaching. They wore matching tan-colored thobes and white turbans wrapped around their heads. They were dark-skinned and muscular like their dad; only Tahani and Hadi took after their mother. All of them had full beards that grazed their collar bones.

"What's up, ISIS?" Tahani said under her breath.

"What did you say?" her third brother Shaheed asked as he walked up.

"I said, don't y'all look nice."

Next to her, Hadi coughed to stifle a laugh. The brothers took turns hugging their sister.

"You look...healthy," one of them said.

Tahani rolled her eyes. Her weight was one of their favorite running jokes. They'd only recently stopped calling her Kirby.

"Shampoo girls making good money these days," another one said. "Buying shrimps and steaks."

"I have my own booth at the salon, thank you very much," Tahani replied.

"Speaking of shrimp," Shaheed laughed and grabbed for Hadi's head.

Hadi stepped back and patted his hair. It was good to see her brothers all laughing together, but Tahani knew the camaraderie wouldn't last long.

"I gotta go find the girls," she said.

"They're probably with Namira," Shaheed said. "You're at the table with the sisters-in-law."

"Perfect," Tahani muttered.

The women were seated on one side of the room. Tahani recognized many of the guests. She stopped and exchanged greetings. The table with her sisters-in-law was toward the front, close to the dais. Two chairs on the dais faced each other, with a long table a few feet behind them. The bride and groom would sit there with the parents during the ceremony. Fatima and the girls were already seated. There was one seat left next to Namira, Shaheed's wife.

"Salaam alaykum," Tahani greeted the women.

"Walaykum salaam," they chimed back.

The women smiled weakly as they took in Tahani. They all wore black abayas and tightly-wound headscarves, their faces unadorned. Namira wore a face veil and black satin gloves. She bounced a chunky baby boy in her lap. Tahani pulled her nephew into her lap, but he shrieked and lurched back toward his mother.

"Sorry," Tahani said, reaching to squeeze his foot.

Namira waved her hand at Tahani. She looked around and flipped up her veil. She had deep, brick-brown skin and high cheekbones. "He's just fussy because he's hungry." She laid the baby across her chest and draped a blanket over him. His kicking and flailing ceased when he began to nurse.

"I like your dress, Tahani," one of her sisters-in-law said.

"Thanks," Tahani replied, hesitant.

"I love the color," said another. "And that stretchy fabric looks so comfortable. It would be great to wear to one of our ladies' get-togethers. You know, inside the house, of course."

The women all nodded. Tahani's jaw tightened. Aliyah and Safia giggled in their seats. Tahani had brought them each their own coloring book, but they preferred to draw in one, making a game out of coloring in the same spaces.

"They're so lovely," Namira said, looking longingly at them. The baby was her third boy.

"Their arms should be covered though," one of the women said.

"Aliyah's only five," Tahani replied, trying to keep her voice even.

"It's never too early," the woman responded with a saccharine smile.

Namira slipped her veil back over her face. The room was filling up with people. Wait staff in black pants and crisp white shirts moved around making last-minute adjustments. At the table across from them, Tahani's brothers sat down.

"I guess Hadi's the next in line now," one of the women said.

The other women laughed.

"Well, Tahani's older than Hadi though," Fatima said.

The table went silent. The women glanced sideways at each other and sniffed. Fatima shot Tahani a look of pleading apology. Tahani shook her head slightly to let her know it was okay.

"Insha'Allah," Namira said, her gloved hand finding Tahani's under the table and patting it.

Tahani looked over at her sister-in-law. She'd never spent much time with Namira, lumping her in the same category as the others. Now that she thought about it though, Namira had never contributed to the other's veiled insults of her. She squeezed her sister-in-law's hand back.

The sounds of the band rose as they switched to a traditional bridal march. Everyone turned in their seats toward the doors. Suad was the first to walk in, flanked by their parents. Their father wore a black suit and an ivory-colored shirt with a mandarin collar. He beamed at the crowd, waving and grinning, every bit the proud father. Tahani could tell by the way he tapped the lapels of his jacket and pointed at a few close friends that he was eager for the post-ceremony party to begin. Their mother stood to the right of Suad, her arm in his, not looking at anyone. She wore a black satin abaya with copper-colored beading accenting the lengths of the sleeves, a matching headscarf wrapped tightly around her head. Clean of makeup, as always, only her amber eyes decorated her face, but that was all it needed. An effortlessly beautiful woman whose face waned whenever someone complimented her looks. As Suad and their parents passed Tahani's table, Suad nodded to her. Her mother's eyes flickered toward her, flat and unseeing, then turned back to the dais. Her father was the last to notice her. His smile grew. He winked at her, and a familiar thrill ran through her. It was a gesture she associated only with him, a surreptitious action that had always soothed her.

Imam Khalil stood on the dais in front of Suad and Jameelah in a charcoal gray three-piece suit with a matching kufi that sat high above his head. His snowy white beard seemed to glow against his dark brown skin. He was a fixture of the community. He'd officiated the ceremonies of most of the couples in the room, including Tahani's parents.

After Suad and Jameelah recited the shahada, Imam Khalil launched into the responsibilities of the married couple, mostly directed to Suad.

"It's not her responsibility to cook for you nor clean for you, unless out of the kindness of her own heart. You understand that, young brother?"

"Yes, sir," Suad said.

"And you understand, young brother, that your money is her money, and her money is her money, yes?"

"Yes, sir."

"And if you come home looking like Sloppy Joe with your pockets hanging inside out and she decides to drop you like a hot potato, that's her right?"

"Yes, sir."

"And you *still* want to get married?"

"Yes, sir!" Suad's voice boomed

The guests laughed. Jameelah blushed and ducked her head.

He talked on about the man and woman being each other's garments, covering and comforting each other, and about a blessed union being a completion of faith. Tahani couldn't see her brother's face, but from the way Jameelah stole shy glances at him and smiled into the folds of her hijab, she could tell he was as smitten as his new bride.

Tahani blinked back tears and wished they were for the happy couple and not herself. She thought of Asaad and the two of them sitting across from each other under chandeliers sharing anxious looks.

Her sisters-in-law had confirmed for her what she already knew. Marriage in front of an imam and a happy, supportive crowd was not to be for her.

There were two lines leading to the buffet table, one for men and one for women. Tahani held plates for herself and the girls, and tried to figure out how she would juggle them. Her father came up and patted the back of the man standing across from Tahani.

"You don't mind, brother?" He gestured at Tahani. "This is my daughter."

The man chuckled. "Go ahead, brother. Congratulations."

They shook hands and he turned to Tahani.

"Hey, honey bear," he said. He took the second plate out of her hand.

"Thanks, Abi."

"Mm-hm." He extended the plate toward her while she placed chicken wings on it. "You tired of hearing your name all night?" he asked.

"Huh?"

"Congratulations, congratulations."

Tahani rolled her eyes and shook her head. She ladled lamb and gravy over the brown rice on her plate.

"You know the story, right?" he asked, pushing his glasses up his nose.

Of course she did, but it didn't matter, he was going to tell it like she didn't anyway.

"First time in my married life your mother let me do anything. So you came out, right? We didn't know what we were having—and the doctor says, 'Congratulations, it's a girl' and so, you know, after six boys, I had to ask, 'Doc, you sure?' Saw for myself and yep, sure was. So I told your mother, that's what we should name you. Congratulations. Tahani."

He looked at her expectantly. She raised her eyebrows in a question.

"Yeah, I don't know how to explain it," he continued. "It's just, I don't know, six kids, all boys, and then you came, and... well, it was like that's the moment I became a father."

Tahani blinked back tears for the second time that night. She plopped food mindlessly onto both of their plates.

"I think that's enough mac and cheese for the girls, huh honey bear?"

"Sorry," Tahani croaked.

"It's okay."

She shook her head. He didn't know what she was apologizing for.

After dinner, they sat through awkward apple cider toasts and music that only the children danced to. Aliyah and Safia had long since discarded their shoes and ran around the room with the other kids. Guests mingled and clustered around tables and various pockets of the room, but Tahani stayed in her seat. She looked around for Fatima and spotted her in the line for cake talking to Hadi. He said something that must have been funny for the way Fatima clutched her belly and leaned forward. Hadi smiled, and his eyes never left Fatima's face. Tahani blushed and turned away. *Was everybody falling in love?* She tugged at the browned edge of the lilies in front of her. A wilted petal fell off into her palm.

The girls ran up and hopped into the seats next to Tahani.

"Well, hello, my little party animals," Tahani said. "What brings you to my lonely table?"

"Sitti got us cake," Safia said, bouncing on her knees in her seat.

"Sitti?"

Tahani turned to see her mother coming up carrying three plates with delicate slices of cake. She set two of them down by the girls then rested the third in front of Tahani. Tahani looked at the plate like it might be explosive.

"I figured you would want some," her mother said. "I know how much you like your sweets."

Tahani thanked her mother and slid it away from her.

Her mother shook out fresh linen napkins and tucked them into the bodices of the girls' dresses.

"I cut them small slices. I hope you're watching their sugar consumption."

"Yes, Ummi."

She turned to walk away.

"Noooo," Safia crooned. "Sitti, stay with us."

A flicker of softness passed across her mother's face.

"Well, all right." She perched on the seat next to Safia and rested her folded hands on the table.

Safia moved to dig into her cake, but Aliyah stopped her.

"We have to say the duaa first."

Safia put her fork down and mimicked her big sister's moves, cupping her hands in front of her face and bowing her head. "Allahuma baliklana..." Aliya began. Safia attempted to follow along, catching the ends of the words.

Her mother shifted in her seat and looked at Tahani. "They know the duaa. Who taught them?"

"I did," Tahani replied.

Her mother nodded.

"You should enroll them in Sunday school," she said.

"They're already enrolled. Aliyah started when she was three, and Safia just started."

"Good."

Aliyah placed her fork on her empty plate and wiped her mouth with her napkin.

"All done!" she said with a flourish. "Can we go play?"

"Sure," Tahani said.

They slid out of their seats and ran off, sliding across the dance floor on their stockinged feet. Tahani's mother's turned to rise from her seat.

"Ummi?"

Her mother stopped with her palm still resting on the table. She looked plainly at Tahani, waiting.

"Why?"

She cocked her head. "Why what?" she asked impatiently.

"Why were you always so mean?"

Her eyes sharpened. "Excuse me?"

"You've never liked me."

"Oh, for God's sake, Tahani."

"You never said a nice thing to me."

Her mother huffed. "I can't say what I don't see."

Tahani's chin quivered. "You didn't want me," she said, her voice choked.

"No, Tahani, I didn't. But you were what Allah sent me." She paused and looked around the room, disapproval brimming in her eyes. "I was afraid for you," she said, not looking at her. "The second the doctor told me you were a girl." She shook her head.

"And are you still?" Tahani asked. "Are you still afraid for me?"

Finally, she looked at her daughter. "My worst fears have already come true."

Tahani sat back, stunned. The hot shame her mother's sharp words always provoked washed over her.

"Nice things," her mother continued, her voice heavy with derision, "that's what it's always been about for you. That's what you've always wanted. Approval, compliments, praise. And for what?" She gestured toward Tahani's form, taking it all in, then swatted it away like a fly. "My responsibility was never to give you nice things or even to want you. It was to raise you to stand on your own feet. To teach you to seek the only approval that really matters, and I'm not talking of myself or your father or any person."

"But you always criticized me, you never let me make my own decisions. You always had something negative to say about them," Tahani shot back.

"I didn't criticize your choices, Tahani. I criticized your lack of thought in your choices. You had children with a man who didn't even have the decency to come to the house and meet your family. And where is he now?"

Tahani's jaw pulsed with pain from clenching her teeth. Her throat muscles sang in protest for air. She saw, for the first time, what she looked like, what the last five years of her life looked like, not to her mother or her community, but to herself. She'd convinced herself that she left her family's home so she could live her own life and truth, but it wasn't their shame that kept her away, it was her own.

"Ummi, I—." She stopped. Apologies were useless to her mother. She'd always blinked them away with impatience. She tried again. "What if—what if I said I wanted to bring someone by the house?"

Her mother blinked, face deadpan as ever. "I'd say, fine. You know where we live."

"Okay, well, maybe I will."

Her mother nodded. She rose from her seat and smoothed down the front of her dress. She moved to leave, then stopped, the tips of her fingers grazing the table. Tahani looked up at her.

"Our door was never closed to you, Tahani."

"Yes, I know that now, Ummi."

Her mother sighed, then stood to her full height, chin tilted ever so slightly. She nodded toward Tahani's plate.

"Eat your cake," she said.

"Yes, Ummi."

***

Tahani stepped out of the hotel clutching her phone. She'd left the girls with Fatima, promising to be right back. She crossed the front passageway toward the riverfront and stopped at the railing. A cargo ship passed by slowly. Lazy waves lapped the rocks along the shore. Moonlight reflected against the water in shimmering lines.

The glow of her phone screen illuminated her face as she scrolled through her contacts till she found the one she was looking for. The phone rang three times before he answered.

"Hello," his voice rumbled.

"Yes," Tahani said.

Nothing but the sound of her own heartbeat.

Tahani took a deep breath. "Yes, I'll marry you." She bit her lip, her voice broke. "If you still want me."

The line was silent, then she heard his laughter, the smile in his voice.

"Tiger," he growled.

SEKAI K. WARD

The Postmortem

Father has been dead to me for a long time now, so long in fact that tonight is the first time in nearly two decades that we have stood beneath the same sky and breathed the same air. I have crossed the Atlantic and returned home to Zimbabwe to bury him once and for all. I watch as he steps out of a dented Nissan Ultima that is at least a decade old and has *I Love Jesus* stickers plastered on the front and back windscreens. He is dressed in khakis and a white golf shirt that bears the logo of a local sponsor on the left breast pocket. Long gone are the Mercedes, the well-tailored suits, and the other accouterments of his once lavish lifestyle. Divorce, womanizing, and the passage of time have taken their toll.

Father is smaller than I remember, more fragile somehow. His face is sunken and gaunt. He is an old man now. A ghost of his former self. This fills me with a sadness that is so all-consuming I want to fall to my knees and weep. I am thankful for the two shots of gin I swallowed earlier—anything to keep the onslaught of feelings at bay for a little bit longer. I do not want to feel right now. There will be time enough for that later tonight when I am lying alone in the oppressive silence of my dark room. The numbing effects of the alcohol will have worn off, and the emotions will come rushing in like a hoard of unwelcome guests. They will follow me into my dreams the way they always do, and I will scream myself awake, my heart racing and my body covered in sweat.

Father and I gravitate toward each other like magnets, stopping at a safe distance to avoid getting too close. There are no hugs or kisses. No prolonged embraces. It has never been like that with us. He clasps my elbow and looks me up and down before releasing me from his grasp.

"My long, lost daughter," he says. "I thought I would never see you again."

I nod and agree that it has been a long time. "Have you found Jesus?" I smile and lean my head toward the stickers on his car. Father is ьn atheist, except when he is not. An opportunist to the end. His beliefs and values built on a foundation of quicksand, shifting and morphing to best serve his interests. He waves his hand in the air as if swatting away a fly, mumbles something unintelligible, and emits an awkward laugh. His reaction confirms what I already suspect to be true, the stickers were placed there by his Jesus freak wife, a woman not known for her compassion or charity or any of the other supposed tenants of Christianity. This woman who was father's mistress while he was married to mother. This woman who bore him an illegitimate daughter. This woman who threatened mother's life and her sanity until she could take no more and finally walked away for good. Father tells mother that she will never find another man, certainly not a white man. He says that no white man will want her because she has been with him, a Black man, and has mothered brown children. She is tainted. She is damaged goods. I suppose that I am too.

I invite father inside and guide him into the warmly lit living room of what feels more like a luxurious home than a Guest House. He pauses to admire the surroundings: the broad planks of the hardwood floors, the high ceilings with their wooden trusses and rustic candelabra chandelier. Large windows run the length of the walls. Overstuffed armchairs and couches are tastefully upholstered in striped fabrics and adorned with Moroccan patterned throw pillows.

Fresh bouquets of flowers have been carefully arranged in tall glass vases, and colorful art prints depicting flame lilies hang upon the walls. I can tell father is impressed that I can afford such accommodations. In his eyes, it is proof of my success. He measures worth based on status and gross annual income. He does not believe in the intrinsic value of every human being.

Father never had much faith that I would amount to anything. When I am nineteen years old, he tells me not to apply to university. He says I will never be admitted. Over the years, I mail him three manila envelopes: the first contains a copy of my bachelor's degree, the second a copy of my master's degree, and the third is a copy of the second master's degree that I earn. There is no acknowledgment.

"I pass this way all the time and never knew this place was here," he says.

I explain that the owners, Mr. and Mrs. Fleming, are a white couple who made their living as commercial farmers up until five years ago when their land was invaded by men masquerading as veterans. The men claimed to be confiscating the farm as their reward for fighting in the liberation war. The Flemings were given an hour to gather whatever belongings they could carry before being forced off their property at gunpoint. The couple moved to Harare, regrouped, and built this Guest House as a way of earning a new living. I am in awe of their ability to get back up after being knocked so far down. I say as much to father, who begrudgingly agrees.

"It is true," he says. "These whites are quite something. They always seem to survive, no matter the circumstances."

Perhaps that is the secret to surviving life, getting back up no matter how many times you are knocked down.

Unfortunately, the Flemings' story is not an unfamiliar one. Many white commercial farmers have lost their land and been tortured, killed, or forced into exile as a result of President Robert Mugabe's disastrous land reform initiative. Originally presented as a means of righting racial imbalances in land ownership created by the former British colonizers, the government pledged to buy land from whites who were willing to sell and redistribute it to poor and middle-income black Zimbabweans. The reality turned out to be something quite different: illegal confiscation, violence, and the collapse of the agricultural infrastructure. This led to the steady economic decline of a country once known as the breadbasket of Africa. Once productive farms—growing everything from mangoes and oranges to maize and tobacco—ended up in the hands of Mugabe's cronies, loyalists, and the Black elite with no knowledge of or commitment to farming. Father falls into the latter category. He is a "cell phone farmer," checking on his farm via cell phone during the week and making the occasional visit at the weekend. When I am younger and home for the summer from my American university, I sometimes accompany him to the farm. Other times, father provides vague explanations as to why he must make the trip alone. But I know these are just inventions and the real reason is that he has plans to visit one of the women he has stashed away in whatever house or flat he has bought for them. The farm is in the small town of Norton, just 40kms west of Harare. Father's sleek, forest green Land Rover always felt obnoxiously ostentatious as he guided it down the dirt roads, passing barefoot children in tattered clothing and weary-eyed women carrying babies on their backs and kindling atop their heads.

Once, when I am searching for a tissue, I find a loaded pistol in the glove box of the SUV. Father insists it is necessary protection against tsotsis (thieves) who may try to carjack us or steal the plastic Bon Marche bag stuffed with cash that the farm manager passes to father through the driver's side window. It is the week's takings from the sale of eggs laid by the broods of chickens that roam inside the derelict farmhouse and around the acres of empty, idle fields that were once planted with maize for as far as the eye could see.

***

Tourism has been sluggish in Zimbabwe due to the unstable political and economic climate, so the occupancy rate at the Guest House is low. Fiona, the friendly manager who is heavily pregnant with her first child, tells me that most guests who come these days are in the country on business. She discreetly nods toward the pair of pale-skinned, middle-aged men sitting in wicker chairs on the verandah just outside their rooms and explains that they are flower vendors from Holland. Fiona says the trio that arrived from Geneva, Switzerland earlier in the week are representatives from the World Health Organization. One night during dinner when I am alone and bored with my own company, I find myself eavesdropping as they speak of meeting with the Ministry of Health to discuss the ramifications of Idai, the Category 3 tropical cyclone that ravaged communities in the eastern part of the country and in neighboring Malawi and Mozambique. As they dine on baked chicken and roasted vegetables, the WHO representatives bow their heads close together and whisper concerns of a cholera outbreak and malaria. Suffering seems to be a staple of life in Africa. It is impossible not to notice that the situation has grown particularly dire in Zimbabwe. The atmosphere of desperation hangs so heavily in the air, it is almost palpable. The young women who clean my room speak of high food prices, difficulty accessing health care and scarcity of employment.

"We are struggling here, Madam," says the young man who clears my dinner plates. He is a "Born-Free," the generation of Zimbabweans born after 1980, the year the Black majority won independence from white minority rule. The country formerly known as Rhodesia was re-named Zimbabwe, and the Born-Frees were promised an independent, racially united, and democratic society ripe with opportunities. When I ask the man if he believes the recent ousting of President Mugabe will bring positive change after nearly 40 years of authoritarian rule, he shakes his head, lowers his voice and says that the "Crocodile"—the moniker for newly installed President Emmerson Mnangagwa—is just as bad and that one dictator has merely replaced the other.

"No good changes will take place for us here in Zimbabwe, Madam," he says before walking away and disappearing through the door lead-ing into the kitchen.

Whether it is guilt, compassion or some combination of the two, when my week-long visit comes to an end, I hand the startled looking young man a fistful of crumpled US bills and leave most of my shoes and clothing for the housekeepers who clutch my arm in appreciation and ask when I will return.

***

To ward off the chill of the evening, a fire has been lit in the double-sided fireplace that separates the lounge from the dining area. On one end of the lounge is a wide, winding hallway leading to a handful of in-dividually designed en suite rooms. I steer father in the opposite direction, taking him through the dining area and around the corner where an honesty bar—fully stocked with Grey Goose, Johnny Walker Black Label, and other top-shelf liquors—is tucked away. I slide behind the bar and pull down a bottle of Amarula. The fruity tasting South Af-rican liqueur is the only alcohol I have ever known father to drink. He seems pleased that I have remembered.

I pour a generous stream over several ice cubes, hand him the glass and make a note of the drink and my room number in the leather-bound notebook that sits atop the bar. I pick up the G & T that I have been nursing and ask father if he would prefer to sit inside or outside. He selects the latter. I guide him through the open glass doors leading onto the verandah, and we make ourselves comfortable in wicker chairs that face the swimming pool and a whimsically landscaped gar-den oasis. LED lights are tucked away in the abundant foliage, creating dancing shadows and soft, warm glows that climb the trunks of the trees and illuminate the dark corners. The verandah is designed in the shape of a horseshoe and wraps its way around a lush, open green space. The emerald green carpet of grass appears so flawless that when I first arrive, I discreetly pull a plug out of the dirt to confirm that it is indeed real. I am relieved to find that it is. To discover that it was merely a patch of artificial turf would have left me feeling cheated and deceived. For whatever reason, I am in desperate need of some authenticity just now.

Father and I sit in a companionable silence that is occasionally broken by a dog barking in the distance and the thud of mazhanje fruit falling onto the corrugated metal roof of the Guest House. When I am a little girl, my cousin and I spend hours in the garden of her house in Hatfield, a southern suburb of Harare. Crouching side by side, we pick through the fruit that has fallen to the ground, painstakingly separating the hard, brown spheres from those that are soft and rotting. We pull our shirts away from our chests, stretching the material out in front of us to form a receptacle into which we drop whatever fruit we can salvage. Later, after we have divvied up the mazhanje into two equal piles, we press our thumbs down on the center of each piece of fruit, split open the exterior shell and suck up the sweet-tasting pulp. By the time we are done, pieces of stringy, yellow-orange pulp are lodged between our teeth, and our hands and faces are sticky and wet, but we are not bothered because that is just part of the fun.

Father is staring straight ahead into the night. His face is devoid of all expression. I consider asking what he is thinking but decide against it. I would rather study his profile to reassure myself that he is truly here with me and that this is not just another one of my dreams. This man who sits across from me has damaged me in more ways than I am willing to acknowledge, and yet I still find peace in the familiarity of his presence. I feel a rare sense of belonging when I look at his face and glimpse pieces of myself in his almond-shaped eyes, high cheekbones, and slightly asymmetrical jawline. For so long, I have questioned whether I love him, but, in this moment, I know that I do. It is not a choice. It just is. I cannot help but wonder what this says about me. Am I a fool for loving someone who does not love me back? Or is this proof that I am still alive somewhere in there? Either way, I am certain I am sinking into the lowest depths of misery.

We sip our cocktails, exchange pleasantries, and catch up on the go-ings-on of old family friends. Father tells me of births and deaths and everything in between. He asks an obligatory question about my thir-teen-year-old son, the grandson he will never meet because I have vowed to shield him from the broken promises, emotional abuse, and rejection I endured for so long. Father does not ask to see a photo-graph, expresses no interest in what his grandson looks like. Instead, he enquires about my work and the status of my career. He wants to know whether my husband found a publisher for his book and if he was granted tenure by his university. Do we rent or own our home? This is not just casual banter. I know him too well. He is assessing how he can benefit from the success my husband and I have achieved and what he can offer us in exchange. He is incapable of having a relation-ship that is not somehow transactional in nature. Like a lover who longs to be special compared to all those who came before her, I once thought it could be different with us, but now I know better.

Father takes another sip of his Amarula before pausing to stare at me and shake his head as if in disbelief. He tells me he so often wondered if he would ever see me again. Says he feared he would breathe his last breath without ever laying eyes upon me. He touches his fingers to his temple, shakes his head back and forth, and once again refers to me as his long-lost daughter.

My younger self would have been taken in by all this. She would have grasped at any chance of hope, latched onto the possibility that she meant something to him in any significant way. Since returning to Zimbabwe, I expect to see my younger self standing at every street corner and Give Way sign that I pass. Earlier this morning, I walked to my childhood home and waited outside the wrought iron gates, hoping to hear her voice or catch a glimpse of her brown face pressed up against the kitchen window. I wandered the grounds of my former primary school, scanned the anonymous faces of the little girls dressed in their yellow and white uniforms, convinced that I would see her shooting marbles in the red dirt outside the assembly hall. But my younger self is no longer here. It is a realization that sends me careen-ing down that black pit of despair because I long to hold her and promise her that everything is going to be okay in the end.

Father clears his throat, burrows deeper into his chair and crosses his legs. An indication that the small talk is over. He looks down and makes a show of brushing an imaginary fleck of dust off his trousers.

"I do not want any surprises," he tells me. "What is your mission here?"

I take a long, slow sip of my cocktail, hoping he does not notice how my hand trembles. Father's words are underscored with a blatant distrust that is painfully familiar. He has never been capable of trusting anyone. Those who love him are treated with contempt and suspicion and are pushed to the margins of his orbit until he feels safe and in control again.

"The years are going by quickly," I say. "There are things that need to be said while there is still time."

Father nods in agreement but says nothing. He patiently waits for me to continue, and when I do, it is without anger or accusations or reprisals.

I tell him that I did not want to sever ties with him all those years ago, but felt I had no choice. I had to save myself. I explain that his words and actions and the distance between us took me to dark places and caused me to consider suicide. Father nods again, casting his gaze downward as if remorseful because he understands how and why this might be the case. I want to believe this is what he is thinking and feeling, but I know that it is not. I say that I need him to know that he has caused mother, my siblings and I much pain and that he leaves a great deal of suffering in his wake. I tell him that there was a time when I would have done anything for him because that is what children do for their parents or, at the very least, it is what children are supposed to want to do for their parents. There was a time when I felt a sense of loyalty and obligation and duty to him, but things are different now. No matter how badly I want to feel this way, I do not or cannot, and this leaves me feeling unmoored and questioning what exactly, if anything, I owe him.

Father leans forward and begins chastising me like a child who has failed to complete her chores. He dredges up old hurts long lain dormant, like dead leaves at the bottom of a swimming pool that are stirred until they swirl around and around in the murky waters. He blames me and mother and everyone else but himself for his diminished circumstances. He says that he did not want a divorce from mother, but that she insisted upon ending the marriage.

I flinch but remain silent as he rips open long-festering wounds that have never fully healed and are still sore to the touch. He pelts me with accusations and spews falsehoods. They hit their mark, ricochet off me and leave bruises, but that is okay because there is an underlying subtext that weighs heavily in the air. We both know what the truth is and that this is not it. He launches into a monologue about the pressures of living with his emotionally and financially draining wife. Although he is quick to deny it, I know that father beats her when his patience has run thin. This fact has caused me to don a shame that is not mine to wear, and yet it clings to me like a second skin that I cannot shed. He is a weak man. He has always been a weak man.

Father proceeds to complain about his illegitimate son—the product of a liaison with another one of his women—who failed to graduate high school and spends his days getting blackout drunk. He laments this son's proclivity for alcohol and laziness. He says he is tired of supporting him and cleaning up his messes. I listen but say nothing. Mistaking my silence for empathy, father goes on to bemoan the failings of his daughter, a child he had with yet another woman while he was married to mother. He says this daughter lacks any academic or professional motivation. He tells me how she became pregnant before completing university and married an abusive man with no education and few prospects. After suffering a particularly brutal beating at the hands of her husband, father says this daughter and her children moved in with him. He is too old and too tired to deal with the chaos of young children and provide financially for their care, he says.

Father tells me that I am the most successful of all his children. He asks if I would consider meeting his youngest daughter. He wants me to encourage her to do something with her life. He says I could steer her in the right direction and act as her mentor. He pauses from his self-pitying diatribe to emit a deep sigh and throw a sheepish look my way. I say nothing.

I lean across the distance between us and take father's hands in mine. I bow my head over them and grasp them tightly. I know this is the last time I will ever touch these hands, so I turn them over, carefully studying them so as to commit every last detail to memory. The leathered, ebony skin is wrinkled and scarred from more than eight decades of life. The palms are pink and soft and crisscrossed with lines that remind me of tributaries flowing into a larger stream. The elongated fingers boast neatly manicured nails with pinkish-hued crescent moons just above the cuticles. These are the hands that spread lemon curd on my toast most mornings. They are the hands that steadied my bicycle when I first learned to ride without training wheels. The same hands that pushed me to the floor and struck my teenage face all those years ago. I long to kiss these hands and gently press them to my cheeks, but I know that father would never allow this.

Already I can sense his discomfort at my open display of emotion and the intimacy of my touch, but I do not want to let go of his beautiful hands. I suppose I should feel uncomfortable as well, but I am too drunk or too despairing or too desperate to care. I tell him that I want him to find peace and that I want him to be happy but that I cannot save him from himself. For a moment, I think I might have glimpsed a hint of sadness in his eyes, but before I can be sure, he looks down and stares at his feet. Silence. I realize I am holding my breath as I wait and hope that he will have some sort of miraculous epiphany and grasp at this last chance at redemption that I am offering. I tell him that I love him and that I will always love him. Father looks up and stares at me with eyes that so closely resemble my own. Any trace of sadness I thought I may have seen is gone, only to be replaced with suspicion and mistrust. Why must it always be like this with us? He says it is getting late and that he should go. He pulls his hands away from mine and stands up. He does not tell me that he loves me.

Impossible

Until I drowned, I thought the cinematic life-flashes-before-your-eyes moment would tell me something about myself. Reveal a profound truth I hadn't realized until my final gasp of breath.

But dying wasn't like that at all.

When I died, the moments that flashed by were...ordinary. Disjointed. They didn't teach me anything. They merely laid bare something I had always known: I am too soft for this world. I'm impossible.

***

I am six.

I'm not having fun anymore. The chemical scents of Icee pops and sunscreen clog the air. The sun flickers fluorescent, buzzing like a cicada; that creaky, aching, rocking-chair sound of summer. Playful screams turn Stepford sinister, and I'm not having fun anymore.

"I'm not having fun anymore!" I call into the crowd. I'm at a pool party for a kid I'm supposed to know but don't really know. I think my invite was a pity invite, and I hate social events. But no one was listening when I said I didn't want to go to this pool party, and no one is listening now.

I'm not having fun anymore. These five words are my distress signal. If uttered with enough gravity and the right amount of tears (not too many, not too few), these words are supposed to send my mom running to my aid.

"Tell me you're not having fun anymore, and we'll go home," she said to me once after I dissolved into a puddle of salty tears, drawing in ragged, chest-collapsing breaths like a seasoned smoker because no one told me you can't get off a Ferris wheel after you get on. No one told me the ride stops at the highest point and lets you dangle there while your older sister rocks the chair back and forth, laughing, "What would you do if I pushed you out?"

Just tell me you're not having fun anymore, she said and didn't think about it again, but I clung to those words. I had been liberated. I *could* get off the Ferris wheel after I had gotten on because my mom had given me the secret password. Even if the glassy-eyed ride operator insisted that I could not as I looped past him back up into the sky.

Word is bond when you're as literal and anxious as I am, but my bipolar mom is reactionary. She says whatever pops into her head, immediately forgetting what it was she said. I remembered and she forgot, as the placating words went slipping out of her mouth and into my ears.

I can't see my mom now. I stand by the edge of the pool, trying to peek through the swimsuit-clad crowd of knees, skinned and scabbed. Knees covered in battle-weary Band-Aids, no longer adhesive but stuck on with dried blood.

One of the knees slams into me.

I fall into the water, hitting my head on the concrete side of the pool.

I reach with my toes, catching the very beginning of the slope where the water slides from shallow to deep.

My feet slip.

I sink.

Chlorine-filled water scrapes at my eyes, burning my nostrils and filling my throat.

Where is my mom?

Doesn't she know I can't swim without my floaties?

Can't she see I'm drowning?

Can't she see I'm not having fun anymore?

***

I am two. The room is colorless and shaped like an octagon. There is too much space around me, and somehow not enough. I don't have enough height, width, substance to occupy a space like this. This is a space built for adults.

I sit on the floor, staring at feet and knees, knobby trunks that rise into branches and leaves. I tug at my mom's dress, cornflower blue, the same color as my favorite crayon. The knees of the trees start shaking in the wind, or is that laughter, it is hard to tell from down here on the forest floor. I tug at my mom's dress again, signaling to her that I'm beginning to feel trapped down here, with all these knees. She ignores me, or she can't feel me tugging, or both. I start to cry, and she responds to that, folds her tree body in half, rescues me from the knees. If I stop crying now, I'm invisible.

"She's impossible," my mom says.

"Let me try," another tree says in a booming voice. When this tree lifts me up, he does it wrong, holds me out and away, leaving my feet to dangle in the air. I throw up my arms, looking for something firm, but my chubby hands clasp at empty space, my curl-covered head lolls to the side, and I continue to ascend at a breathtaking speed. He smells like something I almost recognize, like something familiar gone wrong.

I don't like this scratchy, broad-faced tree. He has hard edges, his hands are too big, and I'm not having fun anymore.

"She's impossible," the broad-faced tree with the booming voice says, and I am back on the forest floor, knees pressing in all around me.

***

I am four. My bedroom is cast in a black so dark it looks blue. I can't see anything, but I hear my sister snoring lightly, and muffled groans from the other side of the closed door. I smell something, sweat maybe, and old pennies.

I swing the door open, and the smell gets stronger. My mom is hunched over in a chair, clutching her pregnant belly with both hands. A woman I don't recognize stands near her, one hand resting on her shoulder.

"Mom?" I call out to this nightmare version of her, but she growls, and my voice trips in my throat, emerging as a whimper.

The strange woman turns like something out of the horror movie I caught a glimpse of playing in the Blockbuster down the street. The movie had clowns in it, so I thought it was age-appropriate. It was not.

"Go back to bed." Each word snaps like a rubber band, taut between thumb and pointer, an affront. Tears will make this worse, I know that, but I feel the familiar tightness in my chest, the constricting of my throat, the stinging wetness in the corners of my eyes.

"She's impossible," my mom explains to her through clenched teeth.

The woman moves, blocking my mom from view. She slams the door to the room closed, enveloping me in darkness while I sob and my sister sleeps.

***

I am five.

"Drink your milk."

The sky is cloudy, but the sun attempts to break through. I sit in my dining room at a wooden table, covered in scratches, paint splotches, and resin residue from the maple syrup of pancakes past.

My mom; an encroaching storm, could be violent or a light drizzle—a false alarm.

"Drink your milk."

A tall glass of the foul white liquid sits in front of me. I watch as condensation slips down the side. I dip my little finger into the water pooling around the glass, and draw wet art that quickly evaporates.

"Drink your milk, it's good for you." The storm draws closer.

How to explain to her that it isn't that I don't want to obey, I do, I am a good kid. But I can't drink this stuff, it's poison, it hurts my insides.

"It's poison." The tears fall unsolicited, in big drops.

"Now."

Before the storm comes any closer, I take a brave sip so small it barely wets my tongue. My stomach clenches in on itself.

"If you throw up, I'll make you eat that too. You're impossible."

And I sit there clenching and crying until the milk is warm and the sun is high in the sky.

***

I am dying.

From somewhere past, present, and future, I hear a muted splash.

From somewhere far away, a slow-motion push of first cold then warm water nudges me, and I sway like marsh grass.

From somewhere far away, a mother's grip rips me out of cold water into hot sun.

My mom breathes her air into my lungs, pressing on my chest in quick pumps.

I come squelching back to life.

"I'm not having fun anymore," I begin my water-logged wail.

"You're okay," she placates. There is a crowd around us now.

"Should you take her home?" an older woman asks.

"I have to downplay these things or she'll meltdown," my mom says to the woman. "She's impossible. If I give her an inch, she takes a mile." The woman nods.

My mom gives me a brief, wet hug, and then someone else is talking to her, and she is gone. I want her to come back. I want to tell her that I'm not being dramatic this time, I drowned this time, I'm not having fun anymore.

***

I am eighteen.

The stakes are raised a little at a time, and life goes on, life gets harder. I promise myself that if I ever have kids, I'll let them have big feelings without making them feel small. If I ever have kids, I'll remember how it felt to be little, misunderstood, impossible.

But will I? Look how much I remember. Look how much I have already forgotten.

I do my downward facing dogs, go to talk therapy, take my hard candy-colored cocktail of SSRIs. But I still have those days when I'm drowning. Days that come and go and come back around again. Days I call out into the void: "I'm not having fun anymore!"

Each time I call out, I hope *this time*, after all these years, some glassy-eyed ride operator finally stops the Ferris wheel so I can get off.

Looking for Papi

I called my sister, even though I knew she was going to tell Mami and then I was going to get a concert of *Ave María purísimas* and the like. Not that day, but whenever she caught the next fever over something I did or didn't do, say or didn't say, according to her. Then she'll draw on her reserve of venom and project a blast from fangs always ready to pierce and to kill.

"You don't even know where your father is."

And I will die.

Because she's right.

I didn't believe in visiting cemeteries and graves, anyway. I found the practice hopelessly morbid and invoking a certain kind of depression that didn't celebrate the love. I'd rather remember Papi when the Yankees came to town.

And when the seventh inning stretch gave me just enough time to get a bag of roasted peanuts in the shell, his favorite. My Papi is in walk-off home runs with the bases loaded and a full count. Baseline seats; I can see the first baseman's sweat.

The kid behind me has his glove in case a foul ball has his name on it. And the umpires are so fucking blind, man. *Idiota! He was out by a mile!*

That's where Papi is.

He is not where I am not.

But I woke up one Sunday morning, twelve years after he left me, and wanted nothing more than to sit at Papi's grave. I wanted to see the letters of his name and trace the bronze as if I were learning the alphabet for the first time. I needed to sit next to him and write if I wanted to, cry if I needed to, and to stay as long as I could. I had so much to tell him, so much to forgive and still more to be forgiven.

The cemetery is nice enough, I guess. As soon as you drive in, there is a serenity not even my cynicism disturbs.

The grounds look as though they could never turn with the weather, sadness or tears. None of the evergreens look weary. They are way too sturdy for diets of only rain and sunshine; those evergreens eat meat and potatoes. Each one had to be hand-picked from an orchard full of excellence grown just for that place. Even the fallen needles have landed perfectly still, blanketing spaces needing their grace.

The gates are majestic and all.

I'm sure the wrought iron finials and the masonry pylons etched with angels are in some architectural digest somewhere. Everything clean. Everything bright. As if something good happened there. The entire place looks like it's been reproduced in real life from the painting of someone famous they'd profile on public television.

Who cares? Papi doesn't.

I don't. I can look, but I don't think I could ever appreciate the aesthetic of the place, really. It's ugly to me in ways the landscapers and the architects cannot remedy.

I knew where Papi was buried. I mean the slope he's on and the general vicinity, St. Andrew's Avenue at the roadway connecting St. Dominic and St. Patrick avenues. The spigot by the twin pines with roots ready to burst the sidewalk is about twenty paces from my father. And the statue of St. Mark is about ten paces past his grave, if you stay a little to the right.

But once I got to the cemetery, I couldn't find Papi.

I was patient with myself at first. My emotion, I thought, made me overlook the grave. I'd over-counted my steps. I might have even been on the wrong slope, so anxious to break my own unwritten rule, I hadn't correctly identified each section.

So, I started over from the far-left edge of the section and walked every row from edge to edge. I read every marker, twice. And when I'd come to the last row, I walked the grounds again, except this time in columns from the pines to St. Mark. The geese, the only living residents, seemed as if they were trying to help, squawking randomly as I walked, almost as if they were guiding me.

Hot!

Cold!

Still no Papi.

I made every effort not to become frantic. Frustration was not becoming of a daughter who hadn't seen traces of her father in more than a decade. I was not allowed, I told myself, to succumb to desperation, to become angry or frenzied in my effort. I was only allowed the emotion and the energy to find Papi.

Still no Papi.

So, I called my sister.

"Where is Papi?"

"What do you mean?" she asked, I could hear the concern in her voice. "Are you okay? Papi's dead."

"I'm at the cemetery, and I think I'm at the wrong spot."

Before I could even get it out of my mouth—*Keep it low, I don't want Mami to trip*—my sister broadcast to whoever was within ten square miles of her, "Oh, you're at the cemetery looking for Papi's grave."

I could hear Mami in the background, she couldn't even get her words out fast enough, "*Eh, eh, eh ...*" her volume increasing with every stutter.

Shouting, Mami said, "*San Marcos! San Marcos!*"

"Oye," I told my sister, "I'm at the statue. Where is Papi from the sta..."

"Well, if you're at the statue, you should see Papi."

"*Este, eh, eh ...*"

"Okay. Okay. If your back is to the statue..."

"*Eh, eh, don't turn your back to the saints without making a sign of the cross first!*"

"Do you see the statue of St. Patrick across the little street?"

"*Este, eh ... ask St. Patrick to help you!*"

"Mami, por favor, I'm trying to give her directions."

"*Voy a poner una vela.*"

I wanted to hang up. I really did.

But I couldn't find Papi. I had no help, no beacons, no guides I could see.

Even the trees seemed like they were bending toward each other and the boughs were laughing at me. The geese flew away. I was standing on a slope in front of St. Mark with my cell phone in one hand, my journal in the other, and shame all over me. If St. Mark weren't concrete, I'd have jumped into his open arms and let him hold me there a while so my feet wouldn't have to touch the ground and I wouldn't have to try any longer. And then maybe I'd turn my eyes to the landscaping and the gates and be willing to see what I'd missed before.

And, I wouldn't have to look for Papi anymore.

I couldn't find him, anyway. Not anywhere.

He was not where I was.

In empty hearts and in empty beds, I made full with my quest to be seen, to be heard, to be loved. Papi wasn't in any conversation or in any listening ear for me. He was not where "Papi, I don't know what to do." Missing from "Papi, I don't know what to say."

And, even on that Sunday morning, when he was completely still and could not hide from me in any way—just as he did in life—Papi eluded me yet.

Unreachable. Silent.

Invisible.

"Okay, stop crying," my sister whispered into the phone, having escaped Mami.

"I'm not crying." I lied, wiping tears from the phone.

"Start at St. Mark but be a little to the right. Face the statue, then just turn around. Papi is right there."

I did. And he was.

I stood there staring at the bronze letters in disbelief; not because I'd finally found the grave, but because Papi was really dead. I was angry the letters looked so weathered, and I hadn't been there to protect them from dying, too. My mind wandered to the funeral when I begged Papi to come back. Come back, Papi, please, just for a little while.

Hands and hugs and tears touching me, wanting to comfort the one who looks just like him, as if I were a celebrity and it made them forget Papi died. I wanted to tell them all I missed him before he was dead.

I sat at Papi's grave for hours until a rustic old man in a golf cart told me the gates would soon be closing. I gathered up my phone, my journal, and myself, and traced the bronze, again, as I've done every Sunday since. Telling Papi everything he didn't know how to listen to in life. Sharing things with him I'd not be allowed to share with his eyes and with his kind smile. And, writing, writing, writing, with the trees and the ducks and St. Mark watching over me.

I sit there, loving my father. Forgiving the man who loved me in the only ways he knew how.

In baseball games. In Sunday drives. In a trip to get a burger and fries, just because. In *plátanos, guandules,* and *sancocho.* In scoops of vanilla ice cream, until Papi discovered butter pecan. In, "The circus is on TV, mama, hurry up." Loving me when he changed the oil in my car because if it were up to me, the engine would have gone on strike. When he was the first man to touch my baby girl, and then had to hand her off to wipe away the only tears I ever saw him cry.

And I see Papi.

He's in every guayabera. Crisp, alert, and present. And in red leather cases holding dominoes kept in cabinets with the good plates.

He's in yellow square back Volkswagens sounding like diesel tankers. He's in whiskey glasses emblazoned with the Dominican flag. In *café con leche, galletas* and *queso duro* for breakfast, every day. And Papi is in my daughter's eyes and in her kind smile.

Everywhere I am.

I don't have to look anymore.

Bios

Vanessa Anyanso is a Nigerian-American writer who is currently pursuing her PhD in Counseling Psychology in a state that's very cold. When she's not studying or writing she's drinking tea, lifting heavy things in the gym, or planning her next adventure. Find her on Twitter @_nessiethegreat and Instagram @nessiethegreat94.

Itoro Bassey is a first generation Nigerian writer and cultural worker. She loves to write about strong female characters defying social expectations. Currently, she works as a journalist in Nigeria.

Jennifer Celestin is a writer, performer, and facilitator. Her writings have been included in Label Me Latina/o, Akashicbooks.com, No, Dear Magazine, The Hawai'i Review, la Revue Trois/Sant/Soixante, and aaduna. She received her B.A. from Wesleyan University, an M.A. from NYU, and her MFA. in Fiction at CUNY: Queens College.

Stefani Cox is a speculative fiction writer and poet, as well as an MFA candidate in UC Riverside's creative writing program. Stefani's work has been published to LeVar Burton Reads, PodCastle, and the anthology "Black from the Future", among other outlets. Find her on Twitter @stefanicox or her website stefanicox.com.

Elizabeth Crowder is a writer, a law librarian, and co-founder of *The Sartorial Geek* magazine. She is also Acquisitions Editor for *X-R-A-Y Literary Magazine*. Her work has most recently appeared or is forthcoming in *X-R-A-Y Literary Magazine* and *Smokelong Quarterly*.

Christine Hill is a part-time Legal Assistant who splits her free time between creative writing, testing new recipes, and trying to keep her plants alive. Christine's biggest goal is to honor her Creator by making use of the gifts He's loaned her...and to buy a home with lots of land in the not-so-distant future.

Nikki Igbo, based in Atlanta, is the Features Editor of Radiant Health Magazine and an avid Black History Month blogger. When she is not lavishing her two sons with an abundance of affection, you can find her appreciating fine art or slinging her locs to 70s Funk.

Lori D. Johnson has an M.A. in Urban Anthropology from the University of Memphis. Her work has appeared in a variety of publications, including Meet Me @ 19th Street, The Root, Mississippi Folklife, and Obsidian II. She lives in Charlotte, NC, but still considers Memphis, TN home.

Michelle Johnson, a public scholar in African American history, literature and cultural production, produces extensive work securing and promoting spaces where socially marginalized people express their autonomous and authentic selves. She writes, teaches, and consults widely on the historic interpretation of Black experiences in Michigan from the colonial era to the present.

Taylor Jordan is an Alumni of Columbia College Chicago's Fiction Department. Between chasing her dreams of becoming Batman and an artistic mastermind, she's mommy to her six-year-old sidekick, The Flash. She currently nurtures her craft as a founding team member of Art In Motion: Creative Arts School.

Ambata Kazi-Nance is a writer and teacher born and raised in New Orleans, LA. A recent MFA graduate, she currently lives in the California Bay Area with her husband and son. Her writing has appeared in Mixed Company, Cordella, and Peauxdunque Review. She muses on writing, books, and life on Twitter and Instagram @ambatakn.

Jesica Lovelace is a published author, lifestyle blogger, and indie short filmmaker. You can find her debut novel "Bad as in Good" on Amazon as well as her four short films on YouTube. Her most recent film is entitled "Her Man." Find her on Instagram at @loveiswaves.

Shanda McManus is writer and family medicine physician. She is working on a collection of short stories based on her experiences growing up in Philadelphia. Shanda is a student at Project Write Now in Red Bank, NJ. She lives with her husband and five children.

Ava Ming was named a winner of the Creative Future Literary Award in 2018. Her short stories have been featured in three anthologies and her writing has been broadcast on BBC Radio and produced for the stage. She's now back in the UK after living in China for several years.

María Elena Montero is a writer born and raised in the Washington, D.C. area. Her essays have appeared in The Acentos Review, in the award-winning SankShuned Photography Art Book, and, more recently, in the anthology Peínate: Hair Battles Between Latina Mothers and Daughters. You can find María Elena at meechiemail.wordpress.com.

Noro Otitigbe is an author, poet and spoken word artist. She is the recipient of the 2019 Jericho Fellowship Playwright Prize. Otitigbe holds a bachelor's degree in Communication Studies with a minor in Cultural Anthropology from New York University. She was an International Theatre resident at the University of Ghana Theatre for Extension Communication Program. Otitigbe's work has been published in Poets & Writers Magazine and Medium. Instagram @noroskoo.

Jasmyne K. Rogers is a native of Wilcox County, Alabama and graduate of Georgia State University. Her soul stories have been featured on For Harriet, Blavity, Nia Magazine, Ayiba Magazine, My Black Matters, etc. Connect with her on Twitter and Instagram @poetic_jaszy.

Ethel Smith has received grants and fellowships from Bread Loaf Conference, Virginia Center for Creative Arts, Fulbright-Universität Tübingen, Germany, Rockefeller Foundation-Bellagio Italy, Brandeis University, American Academy Rome, and PLAYA. She has published two books and articles and stories in national and international outlets.

Sekai K. Ward was born in Nigeria and raised in between Wisconsin and Zimbabwe. She holds a B.A. from the University of Wisconsin-Madison, an MFA from Antioch-Los Angeles, and an MSW from the

University of Michigan - Ann Arbor. She is a psychotherapist and owns a small private practice in Ann Arbor.

About The Editor

Ianna A. Small is the founder of midnight & indigo Publishing and creator of midnight & indigo, a literary platform dedicated to short stories and narrative essays by Black women writers. m&i is her love letter to Black women like herself, who long to reach the pinnacle of their purpose.

A media marketing executive, Ms. Small has 20+ years of experience developing partnerships, distribution and content marketing initiatives for entertainment brands including BET, Disney Channel, ESPN, ABC, FX, VH1, MTV, HOT97, and more. As the executive editor of midnight & indigo, she oversees editorial and creative direction for the digital and print platforms.

An avid fan of Black and South Asian literature, British television, and all things Jesus + The Golden Girls + Michelle Obama + cultural food documentaries, she dreams of one day running midnight & indigo from a lounge chair overlooking the archipelagos of her happy place, Santorini.

Ms. Small is a proud graduate of Syracuse University, daughter to Nadia, and mother of an amazing son, Jalen Anthony, who is simply: her reason.